MISS PIRATE

Diane L. Moors

Contents

James Richardson, Earl of Winchester, has returned home to London, after seven years of sailing as a privateer. His travels have been cut short by the death of his father, making him the new Earl. But in order to keep the title , James must marry within a month . This is the task set by his father, stemming from his dislike for his only child. But after meeting the hordes of simpering debutantes, he believes the task in front of him to be impossible. But he didn't count on meeting Olivia Wynter....... Olivia , the daughter of the Duke of Ashforth, is no blushing debutante. At the age of twenty-two, she is still unmarried , but not for lack of suitors. The truth is that Olivia is fed up of the dandies and rakehells who are after her , trying to impress her with their titles and wealth, when all she wants is a man who will match her in wits and should even be a bit dangerous. But when she meets James, can she break through his shell to reach the man underneath?

Chapter 1

James Richardson, sixth Earl of Winchester, surveyed the docks as his ship anchored at the Thames. Not much had changed since he left seven years ago, he surmised. Except himself.

He watched the workers hurry to get their jobs done, the street rats scurrying to and fro looking for pockets to pick, lightskirts flaunting their wares to the brawny sailors that roamed the docks, either drunk or looking for a fight.

His face grim, he turned as he heard the approach of his first mate ,Conrad or Connie as he was known to his closest friends, which included James of course. " Ready Jamie? " he asked, already aware of the reason for his friend's mood.

"As I'll ever be, I guess" replied James.

Descending onto the dock,they began making their way through the people, careful to keep their purses safely clutched close to them, so as to avoid the pickpockets that frequented crowds like this.

As they walked, a path cleared out for them as the aura around them radiated that they were not ones to be to crossed. James headed towards the carraige that he had spotted easily from the ship itself, as the docks did not often see vehicles of that quality waiting around.

The pair vaulted into the elegant carriage, with James paying a cursory glance at the prancing grays leading it, as they already knew where it was to take them.

James looked through the window at the scene outside, one he had left behind seven years ago.... to become a privateer. The view showed him all that he knew would be there, the elegant Lords and Ladies of the Haute ton, in their finery, strutting as far as James was concerned, showing of their plumes like a bunch of peacocks, the sodding lot of them ,he thought furiously, before he recalled the reason he was here, and decided it was best if he didn't think of his soon-to-be acquaintances in quite that light. Sighing, he looked to Connie, only to find his friend staring at him intently.

"It will be alright , James . How hard could it be to find a bride ? You have a month after all! They can't all be that bad! And you have the title now, that is certainly a great lure , is it not?" James noted that Connie did not mention looks in his description, just the bloody title.

But that was own doing wasn't it? The scar that stretched from his left eyebrow to his cheek was proof that his looks were out of the question, as he had repeated constantly to his friend. But to find a bride in a month? That, he thought , would take some planning on his behalf.

Suddenly the carriage came to a stop in front of a two story building , whose sign read 'White and Smith, solicitors' . James alighted , instructing the driver to wait.

He and Connie entered the building and were immediately ushered into the offices of Mr. White. The elderly solicitor welcomed James with a brief smile. "My lord, welcome. I am sorry for your loss. Your father had left his will and the letter that i sent on his death to you."He paused, slightly uncomfortable about the terms of the letter.

" You must already have read the details of the estates and other properties left to you by your father. Your residence in London, Winchester House has been prepared for you. If you require anything else, anything at all, feel free to send a letter to me , or even pay a visit. I am at your service."

At James's silence the man queried,"Are there any questions on your mind , my Lord?"

At the negative shake of his client's head, the solicitor nodded and said hesitantly, " Its good to have you back James. And I am sure you also know about .... the umm ... necessity of acquiring a bride in a month?"

This time James's voice was almost curt in his reply," Most certainly John. After all , that was the only thing my father mentioned in his letter, is it not?"

The elderly man flushed red as he was reminded about his deceased client's attitude towards his only child. " I really am sorry James, but he was most adamant about it."

"It is not your fault John." said James .

No one could be blamed for his father's dislike of him, except maybe James himself. But he shook himself from those thoughts as he rose and offered the man his hand.

As John watched James carriage drive away, he wondered what could help this dear boy to revert to his old self. Maybe marriage, he thought with a tiny smile. Maybe the deceased Earl's wishes might actually have a positive outcome.

****

James travelled alone to Winchester House, after saying farewell to Connie, who had left for his own bachelor residence soon after visiting the solicitor.

James stared at his childhood home as the memories flooded back. The door was opened by the elderly butler , Hawke, who had been a better father to James than his own. James embraced the old man as soon as the door closed, as he couldn't help but feel happy at seeing him.

"Master James, welcome back! We are glad to see you again! ", he said gesturing to the row of servants lined up for his inspection. Hawke went through the introductions and James acknowledged all of the staff. That was the first thing that endeared him to the servants. His father had treated them as if they were invisible, he remembered. He wouldn't make that mistake.

The house keeper Mrs.Higgs showed him to the master suite. James had been informed that she had joined the household four years ago, and he was going to observe her behaviour.

She asked him about his preferences , what time the meals should be served and other things pertaining to the working of the household. He found her to be competent and hard working, good qualities in a housekeeper. He dismissed her and went to take a rest after having a bath . After he woke up , around mid-afternoon, he realized it was time to visit his Aunt, the dowager Duchess of Aberlane. She was the one who could help him in this quest to find a bride.

As he had no valet, and also no need of one in his opinion (he could bloody well tie his own cravat, thank you very much!) , he dressed in proper evening attire and rode his Arabian ,Sultan to his aunt's residence Barton hall, which was a rather stoic looking house close to Vauxhall.

His aunt's butler Carstairs ushered him into the Green salon where his aunt was waiting for him, a striking figure in a plum coloured day gown, her patrician features belying her true age. He had her striking grey eyes ,he knew and his mother's black locks, that added to his piratical looks.

He went and kissed her cheek as he knew she expected him to do, and before he could even be seated, the questions began......

****

Olivia stifled a yawn as Davy Sterling, young viscount Townsend, recited his recent Ode to her. Ugh, she'd rather be reading her new novel ! The viscount's poetic sense had been destroyed somewhere along his twenty six years, though she wouldn't tell him that. But mama would definitely have something to say about her leaving, and nothing good at that.

She gave him a polite smile and excused herself on the pretext of being tired and wanting to rest, and being the gentleman that he was, the viscount exuberantly wished her good health and asked whether she would attend some ball or the other. She agreed without even knowing what he was blabbering about , and went upstairs to her room .

Olivia Wynter, daughter of the Duke of Ashforth, sighed. Her mother came into the room at that moment and Olivia braced herself for the lecture that was bound to come.

"Olivia dear, what was that awful thing you did downstairs? " the duchess demanded .

"Mother , the viscount is so timid! As are all the other suitors that visit everyday! I can't just marry someone like that! The man I would marry should be intelligent and treat me as his equal" Olivia was incensed. All the gentlemen that wished to court her only relied on their titles and fortune to attract her. And she wanted a dashing man who would be intelligent enough to actually converse about something other than the latest fashion or ton gossip. Her mother never understood that!

The Duchess sighed. "Olivia, don't you think you are being a little irrational in your demands? My dear, all the wisdom you sprout about equal treatment will take atleast a century to get into the thick skulls of the male species."

But when the Duchess saw her daughter's implacable face, she decided to move onto another topic and thus informed her daughter about the ball to be held at Barton hall in the evening.

"Word is that the dowager's nephew, Earl Winchester has returned after seven years on the sea and the ball is to introduce him to prospective brides . The earl used to be akin to a pirate , you know , and looks the part too, Priscilla informed me ! " A pirate! thought Olivia , thrilling at the sound of it. I wonder what he looks like.....

Her mother left her room and Olivia began preparing for the ball, by summoning her maid, Mary.

Olivia liked looking beautiful. She liked choosing the perfect gown to complement her green eyes, the perfect hairstyle for her sunny fall of hair, the right jewelery to go with the gown, the matching silk slippers, everything.

What she did not like was why she had to look beautiful. To get a good husband.

Why couldn't the men choose their bride on the basis of their intelligence, rather than their beauty and the sum of their dowry? Why were they so shallow? Why not marry for love?

As Mary finished fixing her curls into a fashionable coiffure, Olivia smiled at her and said,"Thank you Mary! I swear, if I had to do that everyday, I would be grumpy for the rest of my life! "

"So you say everyday, miss.", laughed Mary, as she curtsied and left the room. Olivia's smile faltered as she looked at herself in the mirror.

If she ever married, it would be because she respected and admired her husband, maybe even loved him. If she didn't find anyone who fit that criteria, then spinsterhood wasn't such a bad option!

****

Olivia and her mother alighted from their coach with the help of a footman who had opened the door as soon as the vehicle had stopped in front of the mansion.

Even from here Olivia could see that the party was a dreadful crush, which symbolized its success. Afterall , no one declined an invitation from the dowager. She was one of the patronesses at Almacks as well, so all the debutantes and marriage minded mamas wanted to be in her good graces.

But Olivia, at twenty two years of age was no simpering debutante. She was in fact considered an Original in the ton, because she spoke her mind and didn't hide behind her fan, tittering like all the other young ladies.

She walked confidently into the throng of people, her emerald coloured gown , with its lace covered bodice, without any flounces, standing out among the pastels of the debutantes. The debutantes envied her carefree attitude, the widows her beauty, and the men simply could not take their eyes off her.

But , in her show of confidence , Olivia forgot to measure her steps on the staircase, and on the last bloody step, as she later thought of it, she tripped and fell.

Well, almost fell, because just as she thought she was done for, a pair of strong arms caught her around her waist and broke her fall. Surprised, she looked up into her rescuer's face and met eyes of the most beautiful grey she had ever seen......

Chapter 2

James was stunned. He had been walking swiftly away from another Marriage Minded mama's clutches when, just as he passed the staircase, he saw a young lady tripping on the last step.

Must've swooned at the sight of my scar, he thought, scowling as he stopped the maiden from falling by wrapping his arms around her waist, which was scandalous, he knew , but didn't give a damn. The girl was falling for God's sake! He couldn't waste time thinking about social dictates!

But as soon as he touched her, James felt like he had been struck by a streak of lightning. It was then that he looked at the girl's face.

Moss green eyes with golden flecks in them stared at him with unabashed surprise. An elegant nose and rosebud lips completed the look. Siren, thought James, one that the sailors talked of seeing on long voyages, that beckoned them to their doom.

The spell was broken in the blink of an eye, as someone softly cleared their throat. James hastily set the girl on her feet, taking a step away from her for good measure, all the while cursing himself for a fool.

The person who had cleared her throat smiled at James." Thank you , my Lord", she said, obviously recognizing him. How could she not, thought James bitterly, no one else looks like a pirate here. " I find myself in the unique position of having to introduce myself, as you have saved my daughter from a horrible spot of embarrassment. I am the Duchess of Ashforth, and this is my daughter Olivia.", she said , smiling expectantly.

Olivia, it suits her, was all he got to think, before his aunt came up next to him, resplendent in a gown of amber silk. She smiled at the Duchess and introduced him." Ah Violet, it is good to see you! This is my nephew James, Earl Winchester. Olivia dear, I hope you are alright! Now you both enjoy yourselves, I must see to the rest of the guests. " then she was gone in a swish of silk skirts, as she set off towards the closest group of debutantes and their mamas, who were all blatantly staring at the exchange.

James took one look at the faces of the group and with a curt nod towards the Siren and her mother , set off in the opposite direction, his thoughts as turbulent as a whirlpool.

"My, he certainly looks like a pirate doesn't he?", the Duchess exclaimed to Olivia."That scar, alongwith that hair and those eyes, he just might be mistaken for one even now!"

When she looked at Olivia, the Duchess was distressed to see her pale face." Come now Livvy, let's get you a chair to sit on. I'll send a footman for a glass of lemonade. Oh child, I didn't realize that the shock of tripping might overset your nerves so! Here now, sit down. And take a sip of this lemonade. There you go, you look better already. Stay put now, I'll go find your father."

But Olivia was not even aware of her mother's speech. All she could think of were those beautiful grey eyes , stormy with sadness and even a touch of anger. She didn't know what to make of it.

"Your servant, my lady", came a familiar voice, startling her from her reverie. she looked up to see the rakishly handsome face of Matthew Albansdale, Duke Radnor smiling at her with a hand held out expectantly.

Reluctantly she put her hand in his, and he kissed it , smiling slightly when she jerked her hand back swiftly." May I have the honour of this dance? It is the first of two waltzes , I believe."

The beast had the nerve to ask her for a waltz! Olivia was aware that the intimate nature of the dance was what the Duke was counting on. She did not wish to create a scene, however, and it would also help to remove any memories of those smoky grey eyes from her mind, so she let him lead her to the space reserved for dancing couples.

The Duke was a certified rake in her opinion, and he had been trying to seduce her since he first met her at the Hargreaves soiree. His innuendoes were subtle, but his expressions spoke volumes. There were stories of his conquests gossiped among the ton, and many married women shamelessly pursued him, so why he was stuck on her, she had no clue.

"You look ravishing tonight, Olivia", said the Duke, leaning closer to whisper in her ear. Olivia shuddered in distaste as she fought the urge to slap him, even as she replied with a curt " Thank you, my Lord"

But when he said," Ah Olivia, my voice makes you shudder in pleasure , does it not?", Olivia had had enough. She stomped on his foot as hard as she could without grabbing the notice of anyone, thankful that the dance had finally ended.

She had almost reached her mother who stood with a few of her friends ,gossiping no doubt, when she was surrounded by a group of males eager to ask her for a dance, dandies , all of them, who had paddings instead of muscles , and the frills and ruffles on their attire could rival a ladies ballgown!

After being promised dances, except the last waltz, Olivia had been sure not to give that to anyone , the men set out to impress her with practised poetry and slightly funny anecdotes. Olivia sighed, it was going to be a long night....

She was just being led off the floor by Mr. Formsby, one of the better men out of her pursuers, and was anticipating a bit of a rest since the unpromised waltz was next, when she collided into a brick wall. Or atleast it felt like a brick wall.

Olivia looked up at the victim of her woolgathering and found herself staring for a second time into the eyes of her pirate. Wait, he was not 'her' pirate! Ugh , she was acting like a positive ninny!

A slight blush rose on her cheeks as she realized she was woolgathering again." I apologize, my Lord. I seem to have been woolgatheri ng.",she said a bit timidly, under his intense gaze.

James looked into the Siren's eyes and found himself saying,"Just an apology will not do, Ms.Wynter. I would have the next dance with you." The last waltz! What in Hades was the matter with him, James wondered, shocked at his own speech. Now I've put her in the spot to refuse me, he thought grimly.

But what surprised him the most was her response." I would love to oblige you, my Lord." , she said, and with years of practice kicking in, he took her proffered hand and led her to the dance floor.

Chapter 3

The next day James woke up to the sound of Connie's voice shouting at him to show a leg,a sailor's term for getting out of bed.

"Hell's teeth, Connie, we're not on a bleedin' ship anymore! Stop bellowing in my ear man!", snarled James, scowling as he looked at his oldest friend's widening smirk.

"Just wanted to check if your hearing's still good, Jamie ol' boy, after so fearlessly braving the mindless female chatter in your quest for a wife." Connie looked highly amused at his own jest, but James failed to see any humour in it. Connie's words only served to remind him of last night's waltz.

After overcoming his surprise, James had been assailed by the feel of the Siren in his arms. Her perfume, something flowery, made him think of how her skin would taste. Probably would taste -

"Is it true that you were a pirate?"The question snapped him out of whatever spell he had been under, and James looked at her eager face, trying not to smile, almost sad that he had to disappoint her when she looked so hopeful.

"A privateer, madam, that's what I was. Though I must admit, most people consider both to be the same thing. A privateer -", he began to explain, only to be cut off by Olivia, who, bristling at his condescending tone, said in a clipped tone," Yes, I know, it is a captain of a merchant vessel legally sanctioned to attack and capture enemy ships. I am not unaware of the distinction my Lord."

"And here I thought young ladies only read about the latest on-dits and fashion", James said, smothering the laugh that threatened to erupt from his lips. The mutinous look on her face told him he had succeeded in riling her, which had been his intention all along.

But he realized, before she could say another word, that it would be best for his well-being if he should inform her that he had only been teasing." I apologize, my Lady, I was merely jesting" Olivia took one look at him and saw his apologetic face, softening instantly, knowing somehow that the Earl would not often be seen so carefree with his emotions, and she was glad to see him thus.

"It's alright my Lord. It's just that I do not appreciate the fact that the men of the ton think it amusing if a female is aware of subjects like politics and war. Why shouldn't we know? We- " Abruptly realizing that she might be going a bit too far, Olivia looked at her Pirate, only to see him looking at her intently. Blushing, she changed the topic.

"My condolences on your father's demise, my Lord. I did not know him that well, but it must have been devastating for you to not be with him in his last days." Olivia looked at him sympathetically, but was surprised by the look that appeared on his face, before he carefully erased every emotion from it. It was a look of pure anger.

"I am sorry Ms.Wynter, but I would appreciate it if we would refrain from talking about my father." said James, his good humour completely gone. Olivia nodded and fell silent, unable to think of another topic to speak about.

Just then, the waltz ended, and James escorted Olivia to her mother. Without another word, he left the ball and went straight to White's, where he stayed till the wee hours of the morning, before he returned home and collapsed on the bed just as he managed to remove his jacket and boots.

Coming back to the present, James told Connie to go downstairs for breakfast, where he would join him shortly. Connie went downstairs chuckling at his friend's black mood. Well, atleast breakfast sounded good, he thought, dismissing everything else from his mind.

After a hearty breakfast, the duo headed to Tattersall's, where James passed time looking at the horses while Connie went to the brokers and saw about purchasing one particular Arabian that had caught his eye.

"James ! Is that really you?" , a male voice said behind James. He turned to see George Sheffield, one of his childhood friends, grinning at him. James grinned right back." Look at you Jamie! Marvelous meeting you here. You came back and didn't bother telling me?" James chuckled at his friend's obvious pleasure at seeing him. Before he could say anything, George said , "And where's Connie? You dunderheads don't have the decency to pay a call on an ol' friend now?"

James laughed out loud now and replied," It's really good to see you again Georgie-boy. Sorry for not informing you of our return. It was rather sudden, you know." George understood what James hadn't said. His father's death was the reason for the hasty return."And as for Connie, here comes the man himself, why don't you ask him yourself?"

Connie had caught sight of George as well and gave him a manly hug as soon as he was close enough. The three boys had been inseperable in their youth, having gone to Eton together . They had separated seven years ago, when James had gone on to become a privateer, Connie becoming his first mate, while George could not go with them as he had a duty as the heir to the Duke of Carlyne. Now that they were together ,George was happy, as were James and Connie. George's suggestion that they go to White's to catch up was met with instant approval.

At White's, George was told about James's need to acquire a wife soon. George was surprised at this, but said ,"It won't be difficult, Jamie man, you'll see", and promptly began a discussion of potential females for his friend.

****

While James was being informed about potential brides by George, Olivia was recieving a lecture on how to become wifely material by her mother. She sighed, listening to her mother drone on about how she must behave to gain a man's attention, or rather how not to lose it, every few days, had caused her to memorize it by rote.

"Livvy, how many times have I told you, you must not discuss Bills being passed in the House of Lords with the Lords themselves? You must behave as if you do not care about such things, not argue about them! Men do not appreciate their intelligence on any subject being questioned, darling. You must discuss the latest ton gossip, Livvy! Or you could ask about the weather if you recall nothin else! Do you even hear me, Olivia?", the Duchess was alarmed at Olivia's lack of response, she must get married soon or she might become a spinster, the poor girl!

Olivia hastened to reassure her mother." Mama, you mustn't worry now, I shall try my best to be a meek and timid conversationalist from now on. Don't you worry at all." Even though it would kill her to do so, thought Olivia. She knew her mother was worried for her, and she was sorry she was the cause of it, but she couldn't very well change her thinking overnight, now could she? But she must try for her mother's sake if nothing else.

Also, she recalled what her thinking had gotten her into last night. Actually she didn't have to concentrate too hard to bring back the memory, it hadn't been far from her mind from the time the waltz had ended. How she wished she could know the reason why her Pirate's eyes had flashed with anger at the mention of his father. But the one thing she wanted to forget was how warm it had felt to be in his arms, how different a feeling from the previous waltz it had been!

Oh she should stop thinking about that, she admonished herself, she must practice being timid! It was going to be deuced difficult as it was, without her recalling the feel of his shoulder beneath her hand!

But still she wondered if she would see him at the Cavendish Ball tonight......

Chapter 4

Olivia was bored. Adhering to her mother's advice wasn't proving to be as easy as she thought it would be. Davy Sterling, her ardent pursuer, was regaling her with one of his tales of bravery, exaggerated no doubt, if the faces of the other gentlemen around her were any indication. Her face, however, was one of an engrossed listener. Her mind was another thing entirely."Livvy!"squealed the voice of her friend Jane Daltry, giving her a blissful respite from Davy's voice. The viscount was not a bad person, but certainly very immature. Olivia didn't want to be called rude, but she didn't know how to let him know that she was not contemplating marriage between them, as he so obviously thought.Turning to her friend, she raised her brows just slightly, asking her the reason for the out-of-character squeal, to which the other woman peered around her to the gentlemen and said,"Please excuse us, gentlemen. I must speak to Lady Olivia urgently."After this announcement, she began tugging her friend towards the refreshment tables. Once there, she turned to face a bemused Olivia. Her blonde hair was artfully styled into a coiffure, and her warm brown eyes smiled at Olivia. "There is no urgency is there Jane? And thank you for that. I was contemplating escape myself. But how I'm going to choose a husband from that lot is a question I would rather not contemplate.", sighed Olivia.Her friend since childhood laughed at her irritated tone.Seems like a distraction was required. "Livvy, have you been introduced to Winchester? He really looks like a pirate, does he not? And those grey eyes! It feels like he can see straight to your soul! Why don't you look there for a husbandly prospect?" she said, smiling at her friend's non plussed look."We have been introduced", Olivia replied, carefully editing the waltz from her statement. "I'll even admit I'm intrigued by him, Jane, but marriage? I don't think that'll be easy. And what were you doing ogling him? If you recall, you are rather happily married! ", Olivia continued, unaware of how posessive she sounded."Ah, but it doesn't cost anything to look, does it now?", was the pert reply."Look at what?", came a male voice from behind Olivia. Looking at her friend's brightened features, she knew instantly who it was."Your wife has been ogling Winchester, Benedict. You'd better keep an eye on her from now on.", she said , turning to face Benedict Daltry, Duke of Pemberheath. Blond hair and eyes of a deep blue looked at her with amusement dancing in them. She knew well enough that he loved his wife to distraction and had the complete confidence that she loved him as well, so he wouldn't take her warning to heart."Is that so, now? Well now I'll have to punish her won't I? " So saying, he went over to his wife and whispered something in her ear, to which her cheeks promptly turned as red as a tomato. She turned away from him and said to Olivia ,"You must think about what I said, dear. I'm

sure you are upto the challenge. And now, we shall go home. I will call upon you in a few days Livvy. We'll continue the discussion later.", she ended quickly, noticing the veiled looks her husband was giving her.Olivia only had time to say "I shall look forward to it", in the driest of tones, before her friend was whisked away by the love of her life. Olivia watched as both blonde heads wove their way through the crowd till she could see them no more, and smiled as she thought of how she had played a hand in their story.The rake and the mouse, they were, and she was happy for them. But sometimes, a little curl of jealousy tightened in her stomach when she looked at them. Brushing that unsettling thought from her mind she looked around till she found the doors to the Cavendish's garden. Time for some fresh air, she thought , as she headed towards them purposefully.**********
***James took a deep breath of the fresh night air and sighed. Why had he let Amy talk him into this! He had not planned on attending the Cavendish affair. When his cousin had visited that afternoon, he had been overjoyed to see her. But she told him that his aunt had told her about his search for a bride and seemed to have taken it up as a personal project. "James how do you expect to find a wife if you stay at home or at your club? The Cavendish affair is one of the most attended balls of the season. All the eligible ladies will be in attendance! You are going to the ball and that's final!", she had concluded, ignoring his protests.In the end she had got her wish, but only because he had come to know that the Siren would be attending the ball as well. So far he hadn't been able to see her, but had been continuously

followed around by the particularly annoying Lady Priscilla Shafer, who could not keep quiet about her vast amount of gowns and riding habits and even her parasols, for God's sake!There was only so much a man could take. It really had become a pain, till he decided an escape to gardens was in order.So now he sat on a bench shaded by shrubbery in the vast gardens of Lady Cavendish. Well more close to the terrace doors leading out to the gardens than the center of the garden itself, as he was not pursuing an illicit liaison as half the ton was. Still, the shrubs provided relative concealment and a view of the doors to see who entered. He had become so accustomed to see Lords and Ladies alike entering the gardens for privacy, he didn't give a second thought to the figure of a lady entering the gardens, till it became apparent that the figure was headed to the bench where he was currently seated.But by then the Lady had already come up to the bench and sat down with a sigh of relief. James would recognize that scent anywhere."Siren?" The question was out of his mouth before he could stop it. Her head whipped around to face him, and James clamped a hand on her mouth before she screamed in alarm, as her face showed she was about to.When he saw recognition dawn in her eyes, quickly followed by relief, he slowly removed his hand. "I'm sorry, I didn't see you sitting here. I'll go find another bench.", she said. But to James shock, he caught her hand as she made to get up from the bench and whispered softly,"I would rather that you didn't, Olivia." She blushed, and for reasons foreign to him, sat down again.Olivia had been shocked to find the bench occupied, but she had been even more shocked to find her Pirate sitting there, as handsome as ever, in black evening clothes tailored to perfection, outlining every muscle and sinew. Alarmed at the direction of her thoughts, she had tried to leave as fast as possible, only to have her hand caught in his powerful one.At his request that she not leave, she found that she had no power over her body, which felt suffused with heat and she sat down closer to him than she had meant to.They sat in silence for a few minutes, both not knowing what to say to diffuse the sudden tension in the air. Suddenly he asked her,"Would you care for a ride in the park tomorrow morning?" Olivia replied by lookig at those beautiful eyes in which she saw that her answer mattered very much to him, and said,"I would like that very much, my Lord."His spirits buoyed by her reply, James kissed her hand and promised to pick her up at 10 o'clock for a carriage ride in Hyde park, before asking her to proceed him into the house, so no one would be suspicious. At which point they became aware of the fact that he had never let go of her hand.Blushing furiously, Olivia then realized that she had completely forgotten about the ball and that she might be missed by her mother. How the man in front of her could make her forget so much was beyond her, but she knew it would keep her up at night.After she left, James sat there for a good fifteen minutes wondering why he felt like a bungling schoolboy instead of an experienced man when it came to her. The idea of calling upon her had been a pure stroke of luck though, he thought as he got up and walking towards the wall of the garden facing an alley, climbed over it and dropped onto the cobbles of the alley like a lithe cat, before walking off to find his carriage among the hundred parked around the house.

Chapter 5

Even after a night of tossing and turning in her sleep, Olivia woke up at eight o'clock, an 'ungodly' hour to be awake, by ton standards. In any case, she had always been an early riser, even during the first two years as a debutante, where she had stayed at the soirees till dawn. After those two years, however, she rarely found the patience to stay so long, as the shine wore off, and the reality of the members of the haute ton slowly came into focus. The malicious gossip, fake smiles, innumerable affairs of married men and women alike, tittering laughs designed to disarm a person before slandering their name......

Shaking off her pensive mood, she recalled the reason for her less-than-peaceful night and smiled. James. Maybe, just maybe, she had found a reason to stay. She blushed and reminded herself not to call him that while conversing. In her mind, it was a different matter.

He had said that he'd come to pick her up at ten. So she had enough time for breakfast and to get ready for the ride. Breakfast it is, she thought, listening to the growling of her stomach.

Her Pirate was a maze, one she intended to solve. Though she didn't know whether she would like what she found at the centre of it. What would he wear for their outing, she wondered. Perhaps-

Her thoughts were cut off as she stopped at the door to the breakfast room, taking in the scene before her. Indeed her entire mind was wiped clear of any thoughts, for there he sat,in between her mother and her brother, as if conjured from her thoughts.

Oliver was laughing at something James had just said, his blue eyes twinkling with mirth. Her mother was smiling as well, and shaking her head slightly, as if astonished at something. James, however, was the one who held her attention. How his face transformed when he smiled!

His boyish charm was reflected in his grin, and those soul-baring eyes! Gone was the perpetually stormy look, replaced by something akin to pure joy. Even that scar on the left side of his face enhanced his handsomeness. She had overheard some silly girls last night saying the scar made him look scary. For Olivia, the scar just made him more attractive.

She would have been content just to stare at her Pirate for a few more moments, but Oliver noticed her standing at the threshold, stood up himself, gaining James attention as well, and exclaimed,"Livvy! How is my favourite sister? Early riser as usual, I see. I myself am just returning from White's.", making her chuckle at his exuberance, which she knew the reason for.

Her mother took over at that point, saying, "Olivia, his Lordship wished for you to accompany him for a carriage ride this morning.", she smiled, obviously pleased at the Earl's interest in her daughter, despite his slightly dangerous countenance.

Stupid, stupid, of her to forget that he must ask permission from her parents for any outing. If she would have remembered, his presence wouldn't have shocked her so much. She replied to him first. "I would like that very much, my Lord.",she said, noting the slight twitching of his lips, which meant that he had recognized her words to be exactly the same as the previous night.

Then she turned to her brother, who, she noted with satisfaction, cringed slightly at the look in her eyes." Dearest brother, I am your only sister. Stands to reason that I am your favourite. But if you are so concerned about my well being, why haven't you escorted me to any event for the past two weeks?" She smiled smugly at him before turning to go to the sideboard to fill her plate.

"Two weeks! You have some explaining to do, young man. To your father's study this instant! He wished to speak to me anyways, now I shall see that he speaks to you as well.", said the Duchess, clearly annoyed. "If you will excuse us, my Lord. Have fun on your ride Livvy, and don't forget to take Mary alongwith you.", she continued, as if she hadn't just reprimanded her son moments before.

James only had a chance to stand up before the Duchess walked out of the room, followed shortly by the thoroughly chastened Oliver, who stopped only to give his sister a withering glare, which she returned by saluting him with her fork, as she sat in front of a chuckling James.

Silence, thick and palpable, descended on the room. James was the first to break it. "I do believe I just witnessed a master at work, Ms. Wynter. I must say, that was brilliant. You shall now have a very unwilling escort for almost every event you attend, atleast for this week.", Olivia glanced up from her plate at his words, a smile taking over her face as she recalled her brother's parting glance.

"We love getting each other in trouble with mother. She can be so very dramatic at times, you see. Its a pastime, shall we say. And you may call me Olivia, my Lord. Afterall, you and I are to go for a carriage ride, are we not?.", she told him, looking for any reaction to her statement in his eyes.

"Then I must insist that you call me James. Makes it a little more familiar, does it not?",he smiled at her then, and her heart, treacherous organ that it was, did a long slow roll in her chest. Despite the turbulent state of her emotions, Olivia managed to smile back at him before saying,"I hope you don't mind waiting in the parlor for sometime while I wear something suitable?"

At the negative shake of his head, she called out to Briarly, their butler, to show Lord Winchester to the parlor. "I shall be down shortly, my Lo- James", she amended, and it seemed to James, almost rushed up the stairs to the sanctuary of her room.

****

James handed Olivia into his elegant phaeton, even as her maid climbed into the back of the vehicle with the help of his footman. Vaulting into the contraption on the other side of his Siren, he once again marvelled at her beauty.

Her buttercup yellow day gown with blue trim complemented his own attire, he noted with some surprise. That flowery scent of hers was bound to drive him crazy at some point. Hopefully he could control himself till he dropped her back home.

With a slight twitch of the reins, the bay geldings pulled the carriage into the negligible London morning traffic. Very few people of the ton would be out at this time. That was one more thing that James did not approve of. But he should have known that Olivia would be an early riser, what with her going against all the other things he had thought about her.

"I trust you slept well, James?" she said just then, and James turned to her and lied smoothly."Indeed I did." He hadn't been able to sleep till dawn, thoughts of Olivia's face in the moonlight and her warm hand in his occupying his mind. "You had trouble sleeping?"

"Hardly any trouble. I was out like a light as soon as my head hit the pillow."She lied as well, hoping he wouldn't see through it. He apparently didn't as he simply turned his attention to the horses as they arrived at the Park.

James deftly guided the phaeton towards the route leading to the Serpentine. The water body was frequented by many of the ton, 'to see and be seen' owing to the benches scattered around it and the beautiful swans and ducks that swam in it.

Alighting from the carriage, James handed the reins to the waiting footman, and helped Olivia down by wrapping a hand around her waist. Just like the last time, shocks of awareness shot up his arm at her proximity."Siren", he breathed, caught up in the spell at having her so close. Olivia stared at him , enthralled, for what seemed like hours, before they were both startled by a throat being cleared.

God, what do you do to me?This seems like a repeat of the scene at the ball at his aunt's, thought James as he abruptly let go of Olivia and they both turned to face her maid, who said, "Lady Olivia, I am going to sit at that bench over there by the willow. Please call me if you need anything", curtsying, before she hurried of with her basket of knitting, trying to supress her smile.

"Olivia, we could sit on that bench near the water. That way you can feed the birds if you like.",James suggested.

Olivia, who was also comparing the two incidences, jumped at the distraction."Have you any bread? I didn't think to bring any.",she said, even as he handed her a packet with almost half a loaf of bread. They sat on the bench and Olivia smiled at the birds squabbling to get the crumbs she tossed. But she was also painfully aware of the male beside her, the aura he exuded too hard to ignore.

"Why aren't you married yet?"The queston popped out randomly and he regretted it as soon as it was out .But ,Siren that she was, she simply replied,"I did not like anyone enough to consider spending my entire life with them."

He was facing her now, which is why he noticed the slight stiffening of her posture and the tightening of her lips as she caught sight of something. James looked in the direction of her stare and found himself stiffening as well.

Matthew Albansdale continued walking towards them, a smirk on his face. Bloody hell, thought Olivia, the lecher showed up everywhere! Almost as if he was stalking her!

"Charmed, Lady Olivia", he purred, holding out his hand for his customary greeting. After kissing the back of her hand, he muttered a curt "Winchester", getting a "Radnor" in the same tone, if not more frigid. Olivia was intrigued by the barely civil tones of both men, especially James. What had caused that? she wondered, as the Duke left without any word, when otherwise he would have not left her alone so easily if it were anyone else with her.

"You don't like the Duke?", she asked innocently. "Hate is more like it." was the reply. "But why?",she persisted, knowing that he would answer her. "I have heard things about him that would make you regret that question. And I don't think you like him either",was the cryptic reply.

"How do you know I don't like him?", challenged Olivia.

"Because you stiffened when you saw him, and, if I remember correctly, also said bloody hell and muttered something unintelligible after that.", James replied smoothly. Inside he was trying to calm down. The irrational anger that had seized him when that cur Radnor had kissed her hand was yet to abate.

Olivia blushed at his comment. So she had said that aloud! Oh, dear! What would James think? But her thoughts were in vain as he made no more comments, just stared at the water with a shadowed look on his face. Olivia once again wondered what he was thinking, at a loss to know how to ask him.

After sitting there for a quarter of an hour more, James took her to the phaeton and they returned to her house, where he surprised her by kissing her on the cheek and whispering ,"I enjoyed today, Olivia. Save a waltz for me at the Harris Ball, won't you? I hope to see you there. Goodbye.", descending the steps and flicking the reins before she could recover from the shock of his lips on her cheek.

She stood at the open door with a hand on her cheek, savouring the feel of his lips on her skin, watching the phaeton disappear in the traffic, and she knew she had found that someone she wanted to stay for. Even though he didn't know it yet.

Chapter 6

The past few days had been a blur of balls and soirees for Olivia. However she had seen a lot of James in the three days since the Park ride. He had began courting her in earnest. Well, as earnest as he could get, anyways.

Even though he had attended almost all the balls she had, making it a point to find her and ask for a dance, three times a waltz, there had been an aura of a certain controlled restlessness about him. Oh, he masked his features well, no one looking at him could see anything amiss.

But Olivia liked to think she knew him slightly better than a mere acquaintance, and so she saw the disturbance in his eyes. And also the fact that he hardly replied to what she said, even to keep up appearance. Though there had been that time at the Malory musical.....

Lady Malory organised the musical every year, and it had all the females of the Malory clan under eighteen playing an instrument or even singing. The Malorys were a talented bunch, thankfully for the guests, who had to attend the musical if they wanted to enjoy the soiree after it.

Olivia was standing with William Malory, whom she liked very much as he had become her friend in the last year, but their friendship had started as a courtship, and when they had realized they would not suit, or rather Olivia had realized that Will, as she fondly called him, had a tendre for Miranda Smith, they had become friends.

Will just would not accept that he and Miranda were meant for each other. He could be as stubborn as a mule about that. But she knew he had warned off a few 'unsuitable' suitors of Miranda's, and she wondered how long it would take for him to accept his feelings. She sighed. Men could be so dense sometimes!

"Lady Olivia, Malory" The voice was enough to startle Olivia. She turned around to face James, who had seemingly appeared from nowhere at her elbow.

Both William and Olivia greeted James, though in much warmer tones. Olivia looked at James closely and saw the annoyance in his eyes. Why she could not imagine. But she guessed it had something to do with her, so she said to William,"Will, I wish to speak to his Lordship for a moment. I'll see you later?"

Will complied, but not without giving Olivia a look that clearly said 'I'm watching you'. She shooed him off with her hands and shook her head at his protectiveness. He really was like Oliver in that aspect.

Then she again turned to James."What is wrong James?"she said. James answered her with a question of his own. "What were you two talking about? It seemed very intense.I hope I didn't interrupt anything important." he replied, tone scathing.

Olivia bristled at that."My lord, are you of the opinion that I should not speak to any other man apart from yourself? Will is a good friend and- Suffice to say that it is none of your business!" James smiled sardonically at that and said, "Oh no, Madam. Never that. I just oppose you talking to a man like you are his lover!"

Olivia was shocked at the angry ring to his voice, and hurt that he would think so ill of her. Her voice was cool however, as she said,"I assure you, sir, that whatever you think about William and me is false . I request you get your facts right before you accuse anyone of any wrongdoing. Now, I have nothing else to say to you."

So saying she had walked away from him, trying to keep the tears from overflowing.

While Olivia was recalling James weird behaviour and their fight, James himself was staring with an annoyed expression at a piece of paper in his hand. A paper that had just now been brought around by a street urchin to his house with a message that it was urgent.

He read the message again and sent word to his coachman to have the carriage readied and brought around front posthaste. About time that Nate sent word, he had begun to think that the man had forgotten what James had told him.

As the carriage rolled to a stop in front of him, he called out Connie's address to the driver and jumped in. The man set off at a brisk pace, leaving James to think of the last eight years spent as a spy for the War Office.

James had been twenty two when, one day a message just like the one he had recieved only moments before had arrived, albeit in an envelope. The note asked him if he would come to a specific walkway in Vauxhall at midnight that very day. It promised a lucrative pay and an exciting work.

James had shrugged it off as nonsense, until an hour later, when Connie and George were ushered into his study, both having recieved the same note as him. The trio had then decided to arrive at Vauxhall at the specified time, if only to find the perpetrator of the jest and wallop him.

Arriving at the requested spot, they had been surprised to see two men waiting for them. They said their names were Mr.Nathaniel and Mr.Russel, and they wanted to offer each of them a proper job. Dangerous, but proper.

"Would you three like to join us?", asked Nathaniel. He was the taller of the pair, with pale blonde hair and a pair of piercing blue eyes. Russel was rather stocky, with brown hair and light brown eyes. He was almost always silent, while Nathaniel spoke for the most part.

James had been the first to speak after this question."Who exactly is us Mr.Nathaniel? And what is this work you are offering? And what do you mean dangerous?", he fired the questions that were on all three of their minds, to the man, who had curiosly, begun to smile as soon as his first question was out.

"Us means the spies for the War Office, James. And as for your other questions, I shall answer them as soon as you are agreeable to our terms. The only term being that You are, under no circumstances, allowed to reveal your alter identity to anyone, however close they may be or however much you trust them, unless it is a matter of life and death, prefrably not even under such circumstances. You will be trained for this role that you will undertake, and you might have to go undercover for certain operations. this may be under the guise of a totally different reason, and- I might be saying too much." he sighed, looking at the slightly awed faces of the men in front of him.

"Suffice to say, lads, that you have a day to decide whether you would like to accept our offer. And if its money you are worried about, though I doubt it, do not bother. The pay as a spy is quite satisfactory, even for you titled lords, and this I say with the utmost respect. We shall know of your answer,gentlemen, and shall accordingly send word to you. Until tomorrow, then.", he concluded, and just like that the two men had left with a swirl of their greatcoats into the surrounding darkness, leaving behind a trio with conflicting thoughts.

In the end, James, Conrad and George had agreed to become spies. It was a heady sensation, being in on a secret that only the most priveledged were allowed to know. But the rigorous training, boring paperwork and small scale sleuthing they were alloted as new recruits passed soon, as they climbed the ranks quickly and it was discovered that James and Connie were more suited to the hectic and fast paced life on the field of action, while George was more comfortable with the mundane task of gathering information of their targets, that could take even days of patience.

Thus after a year of perfecting their moves, James and Connie had set out on a ship undercover to take care of tasks on foreign soil. They were rumoured to have become privateers, and even had the letter of marque to prove it. They even had to use the letter a few times as their quarries had absconded on ships. Living the life of daredevils, they were content with solving the various crimes that Nate, or Mr.Nathaniel as he was known in the W.O. sent their way.

They communicated once a month with George, but after James had recieved news of his father's death, and his letter describing the need to marry within a month, they both hadn't thought of telling George about their imminent arrival. James had simply forgotten everything else in the face of his anger with his father, while Connie had to take care of the running of the ship as first mate, due to the captains rages.

Now that they were back James had sent word to Nate about some news he had stumbled upon in France. It was shocking, to say the least, but he had not recieved word from his superior till now. Sighing, James sat back in his seat, wondering at the working of Nate's mind as the carriage turned the corner onto the road to Connie's house.

Chapter 7

The first thing Connie noticed when he entered the carriage was that James looked displeased. Well, he had been looking that way since they had reached London, but Connie had hoped that James's mood would mellow, if only a bit, after meeting the young ladies of the ton.

Connie knew James was displeased with the whole marry-within-a-month order his father had implemented on him, but he had also been sure that the ladies would love him. Afterall, he had the looks of a bloody pirate, and if the ladies didn't like that, then he didn't know what to say!

He was average looking compared to James, with blond hair and eyes of a pale blue. Their physique was well toned, spying was a lot of exercise! But James just went on and on about that damn scar on his face that was somehow ugly to him. Connie sighed. Maybe that Wynter girl James spoke so much about would just marry the sod. That'd shut him up for good.

Connie chuckled at that thought. James chose that moment to ask him sarcastically,"What has you in such a good mood today, pupppy?" Connie knew James called him that just to annoy him, and he always succeeded, but damned if he would let him this time.

He quickly replied, "I was just thinking how nice it would be if that Wynter chit would marry you. You seem to speak highly about her, and I've never heard you talk so much about any female before.", so saying he just shrugged and relaxed against the velvet squabs and peered at James from under his lashes.

Heat crept up James neck as he was reminded of Olivia when he had been studiously trying to forget about the Siren. "I did not talk so much about her. And after what I've done, she just might not speak to me again.", he said , and before Connie could interrupt him, he continued," Anyways the reason I sent for you was that I just got word from Nate. It just said to meet him at the Albany posthaste. So we are headed there now. Should take about fifteen minutes more, with this speed."

Connie recognized the signs that James was not going to elaborate on the previous topic, so he decided to comment on the latter. Plenty of time later to badger him about Ms.Wynter."So, ol' Nate replied at last. And its so like him to be cryptic and just order us to come to him. I swear he treats us like dogs, damme if he doesn't! 'Come to the Albany posthaste' Ha! " he grumbled.

As intended, his tirade elicited a chuckle from James."Come on Connie boy, you know you don't hate him that much! Afterall , he was the one who recommended the three of us for the job, right?And look how that turned out!"

"Yes well, I guess I got a bit carried away.", said Connie, smiling sheepishly. James was glad to have him as a best friend, atleast he could count on someone.

****

At the Albany a man who obviously recognized them led them to one of the upstairs rooms. Upon entering it, they saw their mentor standing with his back to them near three chairs placed near the fireplace, where a jolly flame danced.

As soon as the door shut behind, them James spoke."Why did you wait so long to contact us, Nate? I believe I mentioned in my note that the matter was of utmost importance.", he demanded of the man in front of them.

Nathaniel smiled as he turned around."Such impatience, James. I had matters to see to before I could speak to you both, pressing matters that could not be postponed. And I think I have an idea about what you want to tell me. The things that kept me busy these days are no doubt related to your information. But do tell me what you wanted to say, James.", the older man sighed lightly.

"There is a traitor in the Lords. One of our own 'titled' men is a scum.", James said with barely supressed anger. Besides him Connie nodded ."That assasin we followed in France, he told us that, laughing all the while as we killed him. But I'm thinking you know about this already, am I right Nate?"

The older man nodded somberly,"Intel came to us just before your note arrived. That's what I was busy with since then. Congratulations boys, you got yourself a new one! We can't send any notes on this one, since we don't actually know his identity, but a list of people with considerable travel to France will arrive at your doorstep sometime this evening. You have to track him down and, well you know the rest."

The duo took the sudden knowledge in stride, though truth be told, they had been hoping the case would be assigned to them. Meeting concluded, Nate shook hands with both men and ushered them out.

Those two were one of a kind, he thought fondly, the job fit them like a glove. It'd be hard to replace James, though, when he got married. A wife always complicated things. And the odds were that she might be used in twisted schemes for revenge. He should know. Hadn't his Adele been taken from him in the same way?

Shaking off the sadness threatening to overwhelm him, he lit a cigar. He wondered when James was going to tell him about the one month condition. Especially since two weeks were already up.

Chapter 8

James woke up at seven in the morning with a blistering headache and a curse on his lips. In fact, there were several curses on his lips, all directed at the miserable cur that was Conrad Brighton. Remembering the way that the bastard had drank him under the table, his anger instantly tripled. And so, unfortunately, did his headache.

James had never been much of a drinker. Though right now, with the bright morning light blaring through the windows, damned if he could remember why. Ah, maybe because of Connie's propensity to make him spill all his worries over God knew how many whiskeys!

True to his word, as soon as they had left The Albany, Connie had started badgering James about his fight with Olivia. James had blatantly refused to say anything on the subject and surprisingly, or rather, suspiciously (as James would have realized if he hadn't been so relieved that Connie'd dropped the subject) , suggested they forgo the social scene and go to White's, a suggestion that James agreed to enthusiastically.

Upon arriving at the club, Connie spotted George and went to invite him to join them, telling James to ask the manager for a private room, which he obtained easily, and as soon as he went to get a drink from the bar, both his friends marched in with identical grins plastered on their faces.

"Get us both a whiskey, won't you Jamie?", said George, still grinning as he set up for a game of cards. "What's got you both in such high spirits then?",James scowled at the two of them, causing them to drop their smiles instantly.

"Oh don't be like that Jamie.", it was Connie who spoke this time. James was instantly contrite. Just because he was angry did not mean he could take it out on his friends."I apologise for being such a grouch. It's just that things haven't been quite cheery for me lately and-" he was interrupted by George.

"Is it that Olivia chit, then? Connie was just telling me about her. Or rather about your obsession with her. You can't possibly be thinking of marrying her, James? The chit's an Original. Damn female argued with Weatherby about the Poor Law Amendment Act. Said that he ought to have more sense than to support such nonsense . Poor Weatherby almost had an apoplexy, if the colour of his face was any indication. Thankfully they had been at a very private dinner party, so the hostess hushed it all up. I only know about it because I was there, and the hostess was my mother! Now would you consider marrying the young Lady?"

Personally George admired Olivia's pluck and determination. Most young ladies were ignorant about politics and the like, or simply feigned ignorance, but Ms.Wynter had spoken her mind to the arrogant Lord, one more quality that the young ladies of the ton did not have. But he and Connie had come to the conclusion that giving James reasons about why she was unsuitable would make him spill his true feelings, since he wouldn't answer any direct questions, stubborn ass that he was.

And he was glad to see that his words did just that. "So you would prefer to marry a chit who does nothing but talk about the clothing she has, and then goes and buys some more? Forgive me if I would rather prefer someone with a proper functioning brain! And as for Weatherby, the ol' sod-", his tirade was interrupted by George once again, who admirably , kept a straight face, while he said,"So it is her! Now tell us why she won't speak to you."

All through the conversation, Connie had been continuously refilling James whiskey, not making a sound, though he was tempted to laugh out loudly at the way James had neatly fallen into their trap.

James realized he had just been outfoxed. And looking at his friend's determined and triumphant faces, he decided to just tell them.

He told them about the first time they met and almost everything upto the fight. He also told them that he was going to stay away from her since there was no telling what she might do when she saw him. His siren had a fiery temper, he thought, sighing at his luck.

But Connie had said that he was just scared, and looking at the light of battle in James's eyes, George had calmly intervened and said,"If you think that we are going to let you do that, think again James. We want you to be happy, and since this girl seems to do that, you are not going to let go. Besides, word is that Radnor has been pursuing her relentlessly, and I think she deserves better than that."

When James had sighed and slumped in a chair at this reasoning, Connie and George had told him how to go about apologizing to Olivia and managed to convince him to call on her the next day, without even the tiniest protest, which was half because of James inebriated state, and half because James actually wanted to apologize to his Siren.

Sneaky bastards, thought James as he contemplated how he was going to apologize to Olivia without her breathing fire, as he ate his breakfast. Decision made, he got up and went to prepare for the meeting.

****

Olivia was restless. If anyone bothered to point out that her restlessness had begun the day after the Malory musical, she would have cheerfully strangled them. But unfortunately, her mother couldn't be treated like that, for the Duchess had been fussing over her melancholy mood constantly, to Olivia's annoyance.

She knew she was being a dreadful person to her mother, who only meant well. But she couldn't shake off her mood. Her anger with James had dissipated the day after the musical, surprisingly for Olivia. But it had only abated when Jane who had visited her, had pointed out that the Earl might have been acting out of jealousy.

She was a bit skeptical of that thought even now, but she hadn't seen him after the fight. And even though she would call anyone who suggested it a liar, she missed him. Which was ridiculous in itself, but she couldn't get him out of her thoughts.

But the fact that he hadn't apologized yet was indicative of how he felt about her. Olivia sighed. At this rate she might just die a spinster.

There was a knock on her door at this depressing thought."Come in", she answered , sitting up straight in the armchair she was brooding in. Her butler entered with a silver tray on which there was some paper. "A caller for you, Miss Olivia.", intoned Briarly, holding out the tray to her.

Olivia took the card from the tray, and her eyes widened as she read the elegant script.

James Richardson

Fifth Earl of Winchester

She quickly recovered her composure, noticing that Briarly was waiting for her response. "Show him to the Gold salon, Briarly, and tell him I shall join him in some time." Briarly nodded and backed out of the room.

Oh dear, thought Olivia, what should I wear! Something to complement the gold room, she thought summoning Mary. As she started slipping out of her current gown, Olivia thought, now to pull out the ground from under that bloody Pirate's feet! And if that took her the better part of an hour, then so be it!

Chapter 9

James had, in his career as a spy/privateer, encountered the fiercest pirates, cutthroats, thieves, assassins, every ilk of scum the world had; even seen the inside of the dingiest prisons and dungeons. But if anyone would ask him, he would say that the forty-five minutes spent in the Gold salon were probably the worst of his life.Why had he agreed to this again? Ah, the blasted whiskey! If he saw another bottle of the offending drink, he'd hurl it straight at Connie's head! Actually it'd be good to lay off drinking itself....God alone knew what the woman would do next, after making him wait so long. A tea-tray had been sent a few minutes earlier, but he was too wound-up in his own turbulent thoughts to pay attention to it and the maid who brought it in (and stood staring at him for a few seconds admiring the caged beast prowling the room, before remembering her station) and left blushing slightly.Suddenly, he whipped around to face the door, though the sound it made wasn't what told him of someone's presence, but it was the prickle of awareness that went through his body. Siren.**Oli via took a deep breath to steady herself, and entered the Gold salon, thankful that her mother had stopped sending a chaperone with her when she met gentlemen in her house.The first thing that she noticed was James (Ugh!) . He had whipped around to face her as soon as she entered. Of course, she had wanted to stun him with her ensemble but the look on his face was much more than she had expected.His eyes had widened slightly, one eyebrow rising a bit as he took a sharp intake of breath. But just two humming seconds later, he abruptly turned his back on her, and, she wouldn't have noticed it if she wasn't paying close attention to him, an almost imperceptible shudder racked his body.Olivia was at a loss at what to do. She hadn't expected him to turn around. In fact if her traitorous emotions were to be believed, she was sad! Didn't he find her appealing?Trying to appear calm, she put on a bright smile and called his name.********** **Dear lord, thought James, the Siren was going to drive him out of his mind.Hell's teeth, whatever he had expected to happen, this possibility had not even crossed his mind. That she would look so beautiful, so utterly ravishing, not to mention appealing to his baser instincts, it just hadn't occurred to him.The gold gown she was wearing had a low décolletage, showing just enough of her breasts as to remain fashionable and have every man at her feet. The silk caressed her every curve, before falling in a shimmery waterfall from the high waist. The sleeves exposed the smooth cream of her shoulders which longed for his kiss. And-In between his appraisal of the beauty in front of him, he realized that every ounce of blood in his body had gone straight to his loins, making him throb painfully. He immediately turned his back on her, to spare her the view of what she had caused.He knew it was the height of rudeness, but he had to get his body in control .A shudder racked his body as he took deep breaths.He hadn't counted on her soft voice calling his name."James?"***"What are you wearing?"Olivia was befuddled at the words coming out from James mouth."What am I wearing?"she repeated, still confused."Yes. What are you wearing, Olivia?" he reiterated, a bit of anger seeping through."What am I - oh James, this is ridiculous! Turn aro-" she was cut off in her protest."Are you trying to make me suffer for that day, Olivia? Okay then, I apologize. I admit, I was jealous when I saw you talking to Malory. You smiled at him. You never smiled while you spoke to me. I wanted to call the bastard out just because he made you smile. So stop doing this. You don't have to dress"-he gulped-"like that to get me to apologize."To say Olivia was stunned would have been a big understatement. She had thought he would have said she looked ugly or something equally mortifying. Instead he had apologized! And he had said he was jealous! Of Will!Suddenly Olivia became bold. She went softly and stood a few steps behind him, and whispered quietly, "James, turn around please."James turned rigid as he heard her voice so close to him. But the soft plea in her voice, he could not ignore. He turned around, and found himself drowning in the depth of her eyes."Do you like it?", she said, smiling mischievously at him.He closed his eyes and prayed for mercy. "Olivia-""You don't like it?", she said, crestfallen."I do."He almost growled. "I really like it.""Open your eyes, James."Sighing, he obeyed her.And her lips touched his.

Chapter 10

Olivia didn't know what had gotten into her. She knew she was considered an Original in the ton, but she hadn't done anything as scandalous as this, hadn't even thought she had it in he r.But when her lips had connected with James's, she had felt like she had been branded in some primal way. No other man had ever made her lose the 'woman of the world' façade that she presented.She had always been the one who everyone pursued, and that had given her a feeling of control. But what were these new emotions she was feeling? This warmth in the pit of her stomach, this need to yank the male in front of her, one who caused these feelings, closer?This caused a bit of alarm, unfamiliar feelings that they were, and so she was the one who broke apart from the embrace.And felt his powerful hands trembling, around her waist.***How could such an innocent meeting of lips affect him so much? He wasn't a sixteen-year-old lad with no experience! But when their lips had met, he had felt like one.But that was not what bothered him.What bothered him was that he had felt a shot of pure tenderness for the Siren in his arms. The desire was there, certainly, but never had he felt any tenderness for a woman.His hands had wrapped around her waist, as if to steady them both.As she drew apart, he saw the same doubts he was facing in her eyes. Why it felt to him that he had only now returned home, he could not imagine.As if waking from a dream, the reality that they were an unmarried couple in a compromising position came into sharp focus, and he hastily retracted his arms while she turned and walked towards the table on which the tea tray had been placed."Tea, my Lord?"He'd have preferred a whiskey, but since that was what had gotten him into this in the first place, he replied, "Yes please. Milk, no sugar."Just then, the door opened, admitting the Duchess, who was her usual smiling self."Ah, Olivia I see you have a guest. And how are you, my Lord?""I am well, your Grace. Olivia was just telling me about the new poem she read. Byron, wasn't it Olivia?", James said without missing a beat.Thankfully Olivia was quick to catch on. Resisting the urge to give him a fulminating glare, she smiled at her mother."' Remind me not, remind me not' to be specific. Sad, heart wrenching yet beautiful words by a man to his- ahem- lover. Have you read it yet mother?", she said, trying to ignore the urge to laugh at the almost comical faces of the two people in front of her. Her mother looked like she was going to faint, while James looked at her as if she had grown a pair of horns on her head.It was funny really, the way one word could effectively silence a conversation. But she couldn't let it continue, even if it amused her to no end. Pity, that."Would you like some tea, mama?""No dear, I, um, I believe I have a luncheon to attend. At Lady Featherington's. I shall see you in the evening then. Good bye, my Lord. I hope to see you again." With a slightly paler complexion, the Duchess left the room.Olivia chuckled. Her mother really was a dear, but Olivia was bound to get a lecture on propriety for her impudence! That caused her to sigh."Why that poem? Of all the choices, why that?", said James.She had almost forgotten he was there. Almost, but not quite."It was the first thing that popped to mind when you said Byron.", she replied, dreading his next question."Why?"Because she had been thinking of their kiss. Because she could still feel his lips on hers, and the feel of his hands on her waist . Because when she closed her eyes, all she could see were his grey orbs, dark with desire. For her."Because it's the one I read just recently.", she lied through her teeth."I see."She was lying. He was sure of it. But the fact that she was lying to hide her thoughts, was proof that she had feelings related to the kiss. It was a start.And he didn't intend to let her go.But now was not the time to tell her about his intentions to marry her, and honestly he didn't think she would agree with him at all. But she would come around. Atleast he hoped she would.To that end, he said,"I'll take my leave now, Olivia. Thank you for the tea.... And everything else."At this, he took her hand and placed a soft kiss on it.And couldn't hold back his smile at the blush on her cheeks.Olivia managed to look into his eyes as he continued to hold her hand, and said ,"It was a pleasure, my Lord."James let go of her hand then, and smiling he said,"I hope you like them.",before leaving the room, collecting his hat and coat and making his way out to the waiting carriage, smiling like a besotted fool.***

********Olivia too, was smiling like a child at Christmas . Though she was confused at James's parting comment, she remained that way for sometime, and having reached a conclusion of sorts, dashed to the escritoire and taking out a paper and writing a few words on it, she summoned Briarly and instructed him to give it to a street urchin, and the message to give the child.Feeling satisfied, she went up to her room, but a surprise awaited her.There, on the nightstand, was a beautiful bouquet of white roses!Walking towards it, she opened the note lying next to it. James's elegant script stared up at her.I am sorry. -JamesClutching the note to her breast, she fell on her bed, thinking of grey eyes darkened with desire.

Chapter 11

Max Wilkins, or Willie as he was known on the streets, prided himself on his skill. If there was an answer to a question, Willie could find it. If you wanted to gather information on anybody at all, Willie would get it for you. For the right price, of course.If you were wondering what Max did for a living, no, he wasn't a thief.He was a Runner. A Bow street Runner to be precise.The Runners were a group of men, who could be hired for their services. These services ranged from gathering information about a person, to even keeping an eye on their activities.They were very secretive as compared to the police, so if you wanted something to remain a secret, a Runner was whom you could go to for help. They were mostly an honest bunch, but they didn't appreciate it when the hiring was done by a woman .But Willie had no such preferences. That is how he had ended up in his secret room, where he kept neatly stacked pages of information on almost every member of the ton.He had collected all the notes while on missions, and while he had spare time. The notes contained every dealing and acquaintance of the subject. It had helped him many times and continued to do so even today.Ms. Wynter was one of his repeat customers, as he had been approached by her a few times before, to obtain information about certain gentlemen, and she paid him a fair wage when he completed the job, so he respected her.Willie liked the chit, damned if he didn't, but her request this time had caught him a bit off guard. When the missive from had arrived the day before, he had been surprised to see the name on it.But never one to look a gift horse in the mouth, here he was, looking for the information she wanted. When he found the file he was looking for, quite easily actually, since it had recently been written in, he took a paper from his breast pocket and quickly wrote a note to her.Wrapping the notes in brown paper, he added the note on top, and walked outside, parcel in hand. Hailing a small boy sitting under a tree nearby, he told the lad to deliver the package to Olivia's address, where he would be given a coin for his trouble .When the boy was off like a shot, Willie sighed. That girl was going to get into a spot of trouble one day, what with all her enquiries. He just hoped he would be around to help her when that time came. Or maybe she'd just get married and save him the trouble.**As Max thought about the inevitable (though Olivia wouldn't agree with him, she saw no danger in her enquiries), the object of his thoughts was contemplating murder. Or atleast serious injury. To the head. With her reticule.Specifically Davy Sterling's head.Olivia was attending the weekly Literary society meeting at Lady Wiltshire's house. She had enjoyed the meetings until the last week's gathering, when Davy had joined the salon. Seeing as he hadn't a literary bone in his entire body, and that he had never left her side for the entire duration of the salon, there was no doubt as to why he had joined the group. The Viscount had been harping about how the poem 'Wilt Thou Weep When I am Low' was a tragedy, when anyone with even a tiny bit of literary sense in their body knew that the work was a romance. Olivia was trying to control herself from doing bodily harm to the man in front of her.Ugh! Why was it always Byronic verses that got her in uncomfortable situations? Even yesterday with James!At the thought of James, Olivia's cheeks turned a light pink. The bouquet of roses had remained at her bedside last night, their scent lulling her into a peaceful sleep. Even then, James had haunted her dreams. That scar on his face intrigued her the most...... How she wished she could touch it!This pleasantly distracting thought was interrupted, rather rudely, in Olivia's opinion, by Davy's voice, insisting that she was wrong about the poem."I do not wish to discuss such delicate poetry with you, my Lord."She said, just barely managing to keep irritation from entering her voice."It seems that our opinions clash rather dangerously on the subject, and since you do not seem inclined to even consider my opinion, I would rather not argue about it.", she finished, knowing she was being rude, but she just didn't care."Have you read Shelley's latest work , Ms. Wynter? Absolute rubbish I tell you!", he continued, as if she hadn't said anything just moments before. Honestly, thought Olivia, he seemed determined to keep the conversation going!But before she could answer in the negative, their hostess demanded silence from everyone. As a hush spread over the room, she said, "Ladies and gentlemen, I have been thinking about this for a long time, and since our weekly get together has been suc-

cessfully running for the past year, I have decided to hold a luncheon for all of us. The invitations will reach your residences today, and I will be most obliged if you attend. Thankyou." She smiled before going back to her group.After this announcement a commotion had erupted amongst the twenty-odd people in the room. In the discussion, Davy asked Olivia if he could escort her to the luncheon, and having no choice but to agree, Olivia accepted his offer.**************
**Thus it was a grumbling Olivia that entered Ashforth House half an hour later.Briarly said as soon as she entered the foyer,"Two parcels came for you miss. I've sent them up to your room.""Thank you, Briarly.", Olivia replied, but her mind was already on the parcels. So, Willie had gotten the information already. But why two parcels? There couldn't be that much information!Wondering about the second package, she slipped into her room, closing the door softly. On her bed was a parcel covered in brown paper. Willie's no doubt. Where was the other parcel Briarly had mentioned?Turning towards her desk, she was surprised to see another bouquet, this time with beautiful pink lilies, carefully resting on it.Rushing to it, she saw a card nestled in between the blooms. Opening it she read-She walks in beauty, like the night Of cloudless climes and starry skies; And all that's best of dark and bright Meet in her aspect and her eyes.Her Pirate knew how to make her heart flutter, she thought, smiling dreamily. Byron again.Taking the note in her hand she opened a ornate box placed on her bedside table and carefully placed the note on top of the one she had gotten yesterda y.Still smiling at the flowers, she picked up the package lying on her

bed. Reading the note on top, she sighed. Willie was always worried for her.Tearing open the brown paper, she lay down . Reading this was going to take a long time. Hopefully Willie had something useful for her.

Chapter 12

James sat in his study, poring over the estate papers that John had sent over. The estates were in perfect order, just as he had suspected. His father had always been proud of the title and everything that came with it.Though he would have to visit their ancestral home in Shropshire soon. Maybe after he married.Since the two weeks James had been living there, he hadn't changed much in the study. It was still arranged the way it had been when his father was alive. He had never hated his father before he had left on the ship, though his father had never been even remotely warm towards him.The Earl had constantly harangued him about living up to the title, to stand a little straighter, speak a little clearer. He had always hired the strictest tutors for James, monitored his every move.That had changed once he went to Eton and met Conrad and George. They had helped him live happily and not constantly worry what his father would think.Slowly James fear and trepadition had reduced.But then he had joined the War Office.James hadn't told his father that he was a spy, for obvious reasons. But when he and Connie had been assigned to go abroad on their missions, his father had refused to let him become a 'worthless pirate', as he thought of privateers.(As that was the rumour spread about their departure)They had argued endlessly, before James had finally given in and told his father about being a spy. At this his father had grown even more enraged, shouting that James had forgotten his duty to the title. Everything that he had taught him had gone to waste in his eyes. James was a selfish child who didn't even repay him for all the sacrifices he had made on his behalf!At that moment James control had snapped."Do you even know how I've been living all these years? Yes, you have paid for my every need, but have you ever shown me any love? Have you ever been a parent to me?I have always strived for your approval! But no! For you it has always been about the title! Always! So if you think I am being selfish, then you can think anything you like! But I am not going to throw away something that makes me happy and gives me a sense of self-worth!", he had shouted, pushed to the limit by his father's attitude."Do not show me your face after this. You may leave now, but don't you dare come back until word is sent of my death. You will then come back and take up the responsibility of the title. Am I understood?", his father said coldly, and even though James had convinced himself that his father wouldn't affect him, his heart broke clean in two at his father's words.But he steeled his voice as he answered, "Clearly."That was the last time they had spoken to each other. James had left for France the next day, and had returned, as per his father's wishes, only after he received word of his death.But the worst thing for James was that he felt no remorse that their parting words had been bitter. His anger at his father persisted even now, intensified by the fact that his father had left him no choice but to marry within a month.James had no aversion to marriage. But the problem that stood before him was that having a wife made him responsible for her safety. And that would definitely be considered a weak link by any of his enemies.And James wouldn't be able to live with the guilt if he was responsible for causing harm to a woman, especially his wife.Which is why he had been tormented over his decision to marry Olivia. He was attracted to her no doubt, but if marrying him meant putting her in danger, he woud rather leave her alone.But an entirely selfish part of him wanted to cart her off to Gretna Green and marry her right now. But now he had the new job to think about......Putting the papers in his drawer and locking it, James decide to speak to Connie about the traitor.******* ***They had decided to meet in Hyde Park, in a familiar spot where they had always met before.Connie was waiting for James when he arrived."Anything?", James asked as soon as he sat down next to Connie."Found out the name of this Runner - apparently he's been useful to the office on many cases. Information enough to fill a library, Nate said. Thought you could go check it out while I work with Georgie at the desks."He chuckled, "God knows I have little patience for desk work, but you have even less patience compared to me."James smacked him on the back."But I am better at field work than you, puppy."Conrad scowled."I think I am going to let you do the desk work, after all...", he grumbled.James laughed, saying,"Now, now, don't get prissy! In any case, thanks for that. I'd rather chop off my hand than do desk work. Now give me the name already!"Connie handed him a paper , which James slipped into his greatcoat pocket."Well then, I'll see you at Gilbright's affair later. And you can't say no, since Ms. Wynter is going to be there.", Connie said slyly, expertly dodging the punch James aimed at him by getting off the bench and waving smartly over his shoulder.One day, thought James , he would get back at Connie for all of his taunting.But now, he had a Runner to find.

Chapter 13

Olivia was confused.

Last night when she had sat down to read Willie's notes, she had expected the person she was reading about to have a gambling problem, or maybe to frequent establishments that catered to a man's baser needs by supplying women.

But what she had found instead had puzzled her a great deal. Oh, there had been the gambling, but the notes also mentioned several trips to Brighton and even France!

The notes said the ducal seat of Radnor was in Brighton, so that wasn't much of a surprise, except that the trips were very frequent. But why would Radnor visit France? And apparently twelve times in the past year!

With him attending almost all the noteworthy balls........ No. He hadn't attended all the balls! She had just assumed that he did, what with him appearing whenever she didn't want him to.

But how could she verify whether his not attending balls was on the days he had been travelling? Her mother would have a fit as it is, if she saw what her daughter was reading in her room, papers she had obtained from a Runner, of all people!

Olivia chuckled at that thought. Her dear mother might cart her off to the country and keep her locked in her room, with only bread and water to sustain her!

She'd have to think about how to get the information she wanted. Perhaps bribe a servant in each of the houses that had given a soiree to give her a list of the guests who had attended? Would they even keep a list of people? It could be very difficult, and there was a large margin for error, she thought, slumping in her chair. What could she do?

A knock on her door snapped her out of her reverie.

"Yes?", she said, eager to be rid of the person who had disturbed her thinking.

But it was Briarly who entered her room, just like he had done a few days before, with a tray in his hand.

"A caller for you, Miss Olivia.", he said, with just a slight grimace, which Olivia failed to notice, as, at the word 'caller', her mind had immediately thought of James.

Had he come to call on her? The thought served to boost her spirits a great deal. Why that happened, she Refused to acknowledge. But her face fell at the sight of the name embossed on the card.

Viscount Townsend. If she hadn't known that Davy was as harmless as a puppy, she wouldn't have recieved him. But since he was indeed harmless, she sighed and told Briarly to put him in the Blue salon. Maybe the colour would keep her calm.

****

As she entered the room a few minutes later, she noticed Davy standing up from the settee he had been sitting in.

"Good morning, my lord. How are you?", she said politely, going and sitting on an armchair across the table from him.

"Splendid Lady Olivia, simply splendid now that I have seen you.", he replied, causing Olivia to bite her tongue before she asked him if he was well, again. She would prefer he say that when he was delirious, and not healthy.

She had tried to think of him as a husband, she truly had. But he was too soft spoken and timid for her. She would like to stay friends with him, but he kept making sweet quotes for her and she felt pained that she did not think of him the way he so obviously thought about her.

When she poured his tea, he started asking her about the latest gossip as usual. Though he seemed almost .... nervous as he spoke, Olivia didn't think anything of it. It wasn't uncommon for suitors to do that, but for once, Olivia wished that Davy was different. Wished that he was like...... James.

Olivia reprimanded herself for thinking of him again. She tried to concentrate on the Viscount instead.

He had left his tea untouched and walked towards the fireplace. "I have something to show you, my dear. Could you come over here, please?", he said.

Chanting her mother's advice on ladylike behaviour in her head, she went to him, asking,"What is it that you wanted to show me, my Lord?"

Before she could say anything else, Davy whipped around to face her and his mouth, wet and soft, descended on her own. Olivia was so caught off guard, that she stood unmoving for two seconds, staring wide eyed at him, before her brain realised what was happening and she pushed him away with all the strength she could muster.

"How dare you!", the words were out of her mouth before the dazed look could fade from his eyes.

One more push from her, however, woke him up. "Lady Olivia- I- I apologize.", he stammered, flushing red. "I don't know what came over me", he continued, trying desperately to appease her.

But Olivia was not angry. She was just annoyed, and a trifle sad. She wished she didn't have to crush his hopes. But she must.

Sighing she looked into his eyes and said,"Davy, this must stop. I have realized we will not suit. Please just know that I do not wish to hurt you, but I- I have set my cap for someone else.", she said, shutting her eyes, but even she didn't know whether she spoke the truth.

"You are wrong.", Davy's voice made her open her eyes, and looking into his, she didn't see any sadness as she had expected, only .... determination. But before she could argue, he continued.

"Even though you do not realize it, my sweet, we are made for each other. And nothing can keep us apart, not even you. But you are understandably overwrought due to the aftereffects of our kiss, so I shall let it pass.", he smiled at her before concluding,"I shall see you tomorrow, when I come to escort you to Lady Wiltshire's house. Good day, Olivia. I shall look forward to tomorrow."

So saying, he left the room, and Olivia staring open-mouthed at the door, sank down on the floor, as her legs gave beneath her.

How- what-Oh dear what had just happened? Where had the timid Davy disappeared? Where had that new, arrogant one come from? And she had to go to Lady Wiltshire's with him? Oh dear Lord!

Slowly getting up from the floor, she steeled herself and began to plan how she would convince him tomorrow that she would not marry him. He had to listen. He was still the level-headed man she knew, she was sure.

Any other possibility, she would not think of.

So much for the colour blue calming her.

****

James frowned at the building he stood in front of.

It was one of the abandoned shacks in the poorer part of London, inhabited only by people wo had no home and no money. It appeared deserted in the fading light, but if the boy who had led him here was to be believed, his quarry would be here.

Max Wilkins. He wondered what kind of character he would meet on the second floor of the building as he made his way into the shack and up the rickety stairs, one hand on the pistol hidden in the folds of his greatcoat, eyes scanning his surroundings, watchful for anything out of place.

As soon as he reached the second floor, he turned to the left as his instructions had told him, and he asked in a clear voice,"Max Wilkins?"

Nate had told him to call out that way, as it was a sort of signal to tell him that someone from the W.O. had come to call.

"Second door to the right!", came the reply, and James went in cautiously, weapon drawn.

But he had no reason to be alarmed as the man he sought stood before him, unarmed. But that was not what caught his eye.

The numerous shelves packed with thousands of sheets of paper, creating a library of sorts, held all his attention."Marvelous", he breathed.

Turning to Wilkins, he saw the man smiling proudly."That it is, m'lord. That it is. Now what is it I can do for ye? Mister Nate sent you, methinks. What does the Boss want this time?", he said, a little sneer entering his voice at the end. James smiled. Nate wasn't known for mincing words, which caused people to think of him as the uppity-speaking 'Boss'. Still, he handed the man a list from his pocket.

Willie read the names on the paper one by one as he went and gathered bundles from different shelves.James realized he was used to these requests for Information from the W.O., and did not question them.

After fifteen minutes of piling bundles of papers in front of James, Willie said,"That's almost all of them. I don't got one of them files.

One of me clients hassit. This one 'ere - Radnor. Expect I'll get it back in a few days. Will send it to yer lordship then."

But James was not finished. Who could have Radnor's file? He was one of the men James had suspected the most and James would not give in that easily. He wanted the file now.

"Who has it then? And if you're thinking of keeping the name from me, I shall send Nate to get it from you.", he threatened, smiling satisfactorily at the man's pale face.

But the name that he had gotten out of Wilkins stupefied James.

Well, he hadn't met his Siren in a few days anyway. Tomorrow would be a good day to pay a call on her, he thought as he carted the crate full of notes to his carriage.

It would be an interesting afternoon. One that he was already looking forward to.

Chapter 14

Olivia had been dreading meeting Davy since he had left her house the day before.His words to her before he had left had made her even more apprehensive of riding with him in his carriage, chaperone or not. What did he mean, 'We are made for each other'? It was preposterous that he had come to that conclusion when she had never indicated as such!Having spent the entire morning trying to prepare what she was going to say to him on the ride, as she had decided not to prolong his misunderstanding by waiting till the end of the luncheon, she dressed hastily but severely, trying to convey her message through mannerisms as well as speech.Her gown was demure with a high neck and coloured a pastel yellow, and her hair had been tied in a tight chignon by Mary, with nary a loose strand in sight.The luncheon had been scheduled at two o'clock, and Davy had mentioned in a note that he would arrive to collect her at a quarter to the hour. Olivia waited for his arrival impatiently, hoping to go through with her plan quickly.How she hated to cause anyone pain! But she knew that Davy would make some young maiden a good husband, just not her. She was a wasted cause as far as other gentlemen were considered. She had already set her sights on som eone....Though she did not start with surprise when Briarly entered the parlor suddenly, she stood up when she saw the discomfort on his face."What is it Briarly?", she asked, alarmed."The gentleman in the carriage at our doorstep insists that you climb in it. Claims that he has to escort you to a luncheon! The footman is at the door. Should I tell him to leave, then ?", Briarly rushed on visibly incensed at the impropriety of the gentleman not coming upto the house to escort her himself.Olivia however, rushed to windows and peering at the carriage, recognized the crest on the door. Davy was here.Turning to the weary butler, she smiled and reassured him,"Briarly, it is perfectly fine. Viscount Townsend has arrived to escort me to the Literary club luncheon."Picking up her cloak, she draped it on herself at the door which Briarly had left open in his haste to reach her, and preceeding the footman sent to help her into the carriage, which she saw uncomfortably, was a closed one.Steeling herself she accepted the footman's proffered hand and climbed into the vehicle.But before her eyes could adjust to the dim interior, her nose and mouth were covered with a foul smelling cloth. As the strong fumes rapidly made her lose consciousness, her last thought was that she would kill Davy for this.***

Davy stared at the sleeping form of Olivia, as she rested on the seat opposite him. How beautiful she looked even while sleeping, he thought. And now she would become his.Davy remembered the first time he had seen her, two years ago. Like countless other men he had fallen prey to her charm and beauty. The only difference was that she fell for him too.The way she gave him attention every time he spoke to her, the way she looked at him when they danced together, it shone in her eyes, her love for him.But he had known that Winchester would be a problem. The way he had looked at Olivia when he had caught her on the stairs and when they had waltzed...... his desire showed in his eyes.Davy wouldn't ever think such adulterated thoughts about Olivia. His intentions were far too pure. He loved her, after all.But Davy had not panicked. He knew that Olivia would never dream of marrying anyone but him.That was until she had spoken of fancying someone else yesterday. Davy knew he had to work fast if he wanted to make Olivia his bride. So he had hatched the plan for kidnapping her.He knew she would come to her senses when he spoke to her.Just then the carriage came to a halt and the footman informed him that they had reached the inn where Davy had decided to tell Olivia the good news.She had yet to awaken, of course. The dose of chloroform he had given her would last for atleast half an hour more. He hadn't wanted to take the risk of her awakening and raising a cry before he could speak to her properly.As the door opened, Davy called to the footman to come and lift Olivia to carry her into the room he had booked the night before. Rest assured, the innkeeper would not question him bringing a unconscious lady into the inn.Davy posted the footman outside the door of the room where Olivia had been laid down, giving him express instructions to send for him as soon as she awakened. His whereabouts would be with the innkeeper.One hour had passed since he had drugged her and she had not awakened, so it seemed safe to assume that she would be out like a light for sometime longer. He had left a maid to take care of his treasure. She had to be treated like the princess that she was, he believed.Davy smiled. He could scarcely wait till they were married......********************* ** James was frustrated. Almost all of the names in the list of suspects had been worthless. After spending the previous night and the morning poring over notes that hadn't given him a better view of the situation, even the lunch that was being served to him didn't seem appetizing.Drat Olivia for keeping that one file from him! Why she would want information on Radnor, he couldn't fathom.It wasn't usual for him to lunch as late as two in the afternoon. But it was also not like him to have a fitful sleep worrying about a woman's well being. But he had slept poorly, worried whether Olivia was meddling in some dangerous activity that she should have left alone.Thinking about that made him panic. He should go to her right now and demand her to tell him why she had the file in her possession.Firming his resolve, James got up from the dining table, grabbing his greatcoat from his study before striding towards the stables to saddle Sultan.Within minutes he was off.**"She left the house a quarter of an hour back, my Lord. Viscount Townsend's carriage had come to escort her to the Literary club luncheon.", Olivia's butler, Briarly was telling James, whose mind had formed a cold shield to protect itself from the anxiety that threatened to consume him. But something about the man's sentence seemed wrong to James."You said that the viscount's carriage had come for Olivia. Didn't the Viscount himself escort her?", he said."No, my Lord. The Viscount didn't deign fit to come into the house personally to take Miss Olivia out. But when she saw the carriage, Miss Olivia had gone with the footman that had come to the door."Briarly said, continuing thoughtfully, "Though now that your lordship mentions it, My Lady had been a trifle disconcerted when she had seen the carriage, and she had been mumbling to herself, which she only does when she is apprehensive about something."No sooner had Briarly finished his sentence James had turned on his heel and marched down the steps of Olivia's house to Sultan, and taking the reigns from the boy holding them, mounted the saddle and headed to Lady Wiltshire's home. If only he could see his Siren, this feeling in the pit of his stomach would go away.When he arrived at Lady Wiltshire's, the butler had informed him that Olivia had not arrived for the luncheon. And neither had the Viscount.James had wasted no time in going to Olivia's house again, this time to speak to her father."What seems to be the problem Winchester ?", said the Duke of Ashforth, unsmiling, as he took in the look on James face.As quickly as possible, James summarized the story as he knew it, leaving out the part about Radnor's file. Better not to get more people involved, he thought."Townsend! But Olivia would never go willingly with that sod!", thundered Oliver, who had also been in his father's study when James had arrived."Then it must be without her consent."The Duke was the calmest of the three, but inside the rage boiled . "I cannot let him marry her. We must be quick to locate her. There are about three ways that Townsend would think to take her, which would lead to his country home. Will you help us Winchester?", he said, knowing that the answer was crucial."Yes."The reply was curt. "But I would have your blessing to marry your daughter by special license, if I am to find her. If either of you finds her, I shall marry her in a weeks time.",James words stunned the Duke for all of two seconds, before he made up his mind."You have it. Now lets go hunt that addle-brained hare." He concluded, and all three males set off in separate carriages, James having sent a footman for his carriage and to return Sultan home.As he sat in the confines of the carriage which was going at a fast pace, James hoped he wasn't too late.Because he couldn't live with the thought of his Siren in another man's arms.

Chapter 15

When Olivia first awoke, she had panicked slightly as she took in the unfamiliar surroundings.The room was small, but not tiny. The bed she was sleeping in was comfortable, and she was covered in blankets......... Dear Lord!What was she doing in a bed ? No, it couldn't be Davy! She prayed fervently as the day's events came back full force. No, that couldn't have happened.Besides, wouldn't she feel different if that had happened. And she wasn't feeling anything but a bit queasy, which must be the effects of that chloroform she had inhaled.That scoundrel Davy! Just wait till he comes back! She'd skin his hide! How dare he do this to her! She had never, in her wildest imaginations, thought that he could stoop so low.On the heels of that thought came another, far more shocking than the first.Would she have to marry Davy? How long had it been since she had lost consciousness? Where was she? Dear God, what would mama and papa say!Mind whirling with these questions, she sat up, pushing the blankets off her body. But then she noticed the young maid in the room, who immediately rushed to her side."My lady, are you alright? Would you like to eat anything? Water to wash? A bath?

Perhaps-", she was cut off mid-sentence by a very irritated Olivia."I wish to leave this chamber at once! Where is my cloak?", she said, though she soon spotted the cloak on a nearby chair and rushed to it, putting it on swiftly."My lady you cannot leave! The door-"But Olivia had already begun pulling on it, when someone on the outside pushed it open and she fell down in an undignified heap, with a loud "Ah" erupting from her lips. But she soon shut her mouth when she noticed the burly man standing in the doorway. He sneered at her."Ah, so ye's the lady that the fancy Lord wants to keep locked in 'ere! A fine specimen indeed! 'tis no wonder he paid a pretty price for me to keep ye safe! Now, there'll be no 'leaving this chamber' anytime soon for ye missy! Ye'd do best to go and sit nice and quiet on that chair there, see? One shout from Betsy here and I'll tie ye to the bed! ", so saying he gave her a menacing stare, promptly shutting the door, before Olivia could even say anything!Olivia was tempted to jump out of the window, Betsy was a tiny thing and couldn't stop her from doing that. But she couldn't risk that big brute outside coming in as soon as the girl called for help. Dash it all! She couldn't think of anything but trying to convince Davy that he was making a mistake. But he wasn't even here yet! How could she speak to him if he didn't come to her?Resisting the urge to pull her hair, she quietly asked the maid what the time was."Three o'clock, my Lady.", she replied timidly, after looking at the rusty timepiece dangling from the waist of her gown.Just more than an hour since she had left home, sighed Olivia. The thought brought a pang to her chest.What if she was forced to marry Davy? She could not marry him. Why? Because he didn't make her happy, didn't make her heart swell in her breast, didn't make her long for his kisses, like.......James. She now realized how much she was attracted to him, how one look from those grey eyes could turn her into mush, how much she longed for his touch. She could not bear it if he married some other woman. She wanted to marry him! She had never felt this way about any other gentleman and she would not lose him because of Davy!The thought gave her courage. She would scream at Davy to stop this foolishness. She did not wish to marry him. She would not marry him. Maybe, after all her cajoling had failed, the plain truth would awaken him.Steeling herself for the confrontation, she sat on a chair facing the door, and pondered her plan of attack.** **************************Davy walked down the hallway towards the room where his future wife waited. The temporary footman, actually a hired thug, had sent word a few minutes before, claiming that she was awake. Davy had wasted no time in leaving what he was doing halfway before rushing to meet Olivia.He dismissed the man standing at the door, paying him the fee he had promised, before opening the door and entering.He noticed Olivia sitting in one of the chairs, an unreadable expression on her face. She must be waiting for me to tell the maid to leave, he thought, marveling at the thought that she did not order the maid herself, but waited for him to do so. She would make him an obedient wife, he thought, smiling at her. She did not smile back.When the maid, who had been paid earlier, left, he closed the door and turned to face her with a bright smile."Olivia-""I shall not marry you."Davy was shocked at her words. But he tried to reason with her. "My dear, of course you are going to marry me! That is why you are here.""No. I am here because you abducted me. Davy, you must understand! I like you, I truly do, but I cannot in good conscience marry you! I don't lo-""Don't say that! You do love me Olivia, as I love you! We are made for each other, don't you see! All those conversations, those dances, they were proof of your love!", Davy reiterated, voice slightly hysterical. He could not afford to lose her now! He must tell her-Just then the door opened with such force, it knocked into the wall with a resounding 'crack!'.Davy turned towards it, and almost collapsed to the floor, horrified at the sight before him.***James was beyond furious. It had started as a mild anger, but had quickly escalated as he reached the inn where Olivia had been taken.He was angry because it had been so easy to find the place where she had been taken to. A few coins slipped into the right pockets, and all the story spilled out. He could only hope that the wagging tongues he had paid to talk as well as keep quiet about the whole story, would not spread the tale anywhere else.Townsend had been foolish enough not to take any extra precautions to prevent scandal, taking Olivia to the first high quality inn on the road to his country house. His carriage had stood proudly at the front of the inn, proclaiming his arrival. James had sent the carriage away to the back of the establishment, seething with anger.If the bastard had done anything to Olivia, he'd kill him. As it is he was going to call him out over this matter. He didn't want to have to kill him.In a matter of minutes, he had the information he was looking for, after threatening the innkeeper. He pushed the door open with all his strength, expecting it to be locked. But it swung inwards without protest, crashing onto the wall.James looked at the two faces before him. Townsend looked as if he was about to faint. And Olivia looked like...... well frankly he could not tell what she looked like. It seemed like a mixture between relief and anger, but he could not be sure. He almost laughed. Leave it to his Siren to be angry at him at a time like this!"I have come for Lady Olivia, Townsend.", and at the look on the other man's face he continued, "You'd do well not to protest about it, puppy. I do not wish to harm you right now. As it is my seconds shall call on you tonight. Make yourself available for a dawn appointment."James watched with satisfaction as the blood drained from the Viscount's face, giving it an ashen pallor. But his thoughts were interrupted by Olivia saying one word."No.""What?", he asked, incredulous."I said that you shall not have a dawn appointment.", she stated clearly, not even flinching at his glare."You should at least wait till we are married to start ordering me around."Now it was Olivia's face that lost all of it's angry colour as she stared at him, dumbstruck. Had he just said 'married'? Her brain could not get past that, but she had important things to take care of.Davy would not survive in a duel with James. And even though she was angry with him for bringing her here, she did not want him to die. Which she was sure would happen if he accepted the challenge James had put to him. And he would accept, she knew that. Why? Because he was a male. A stupid, egotistical, addle-brained male!Everything had to be solved by a duel or some show of their strength. And she was tired of it!"You shall not have a dawn appointment, my Lord. And that is the last thing I shall say about it!", she said marching out of the door, head high.She walked down the stairs, and with just a disgusted look at the innkeeper, who was still frozen with fear at James threats, left the inn. But when she stepped outside the inn, she realized she was without money for conveyance. Her reticule had been lost, perhaps in Davy's carriage, and she had nothing except her cloak. Her only chance to go back home was James. The very one that she had left in a room inside while proclaiming that he would not have a dawn appointment.Ah! She was such a fool sometimes! Why would he even listen to her? And he was .... Alone in a room with Davy! Oh dear! He must have killed him by now! But before she could rush into the inn, she collided with a hard male body. James."Where is Davy? Is he okay? Why is he not with you? Why-", her questions were cut off as James dragged her close to him and crushed his lips to hers.All thoughts of Davy's welfare flew out of Olivia's mind as she felt James lips slant hungrily over her own. She felt his desire in the kiss, but there was a hint of ... anger? He was angry at her? Just then, he bit her lip and she gasped, and he took the opportunity to plunge his tongue into her mouth. Olivia felt like she had been set aflame. James tongue did unthinkable things to her mouth, making her feel a rush of heat at her center. But just as the kiss became more heated, James set her down abruptly, breathing ragged.As James stared at the temptress in front of him, breathing heavily and eyes dark with desire, he berated himself for his behavior. But since he had seen her in the room with Townsend, not seeming like she wanted to escape the man, he had wanted to mark her as his. There had been a primitive rush flowing through his veins, one he had tried to control, but when she had begun asking about 'Davy' after colliding with him, he had lost whatever control he had.He began to tell her that they would be going to Benham Park, his country house, for their marriage.And saw her eyes roll back in her head as she fainted.

Traitor

He rolled off the satisfied and panting body of the whore, walking towards the chair on which his robe had been laid. After putting it on and belting it closed, he turned to the now empty bed. The whores had learned not to linger after he left them. He did not appreciate it, and it brought them a round of whipping which they would rather avoid.Walking to the study, where a light had been left burning on his orders, he poured some brandy from the decanter and settled down at his desk, where papers had been scattered earl ier.He had to say, the French paid well. Their plans of action, like the ones in front of him were precise and ruthless. Two qualities he appreciated a great deal.His lips twisted as he read the name of his current assignment. James Richardson. Bastard should have died that day when my dagger scarred his face, he thought, anger boiling in his chest. Would have died if that accomplice of his wasn't there to outnumber him. Conrad Brighton. He would take care of that later. Now James was his target.He had observed him today, dashing from one house to the next, and had laughed at his discomfort. He knew about the Wynter chit of course. Even about how Winchester was besotted with the wench. After all he was the one who put the idea of abducting her to that sod Townsend, when he had found him lying foxed at that gaming hell. It had been pure luck, finding him there. And the boy was deep enough in his cups to actually plan the thing and go through with it, he thought chuckling to himself. What fools love made of men!He himself would never understand it. When his gambling father had killed himself with his own pistol, his mother had withered away as well, illness taking her a few years after her husband. But he had been left to pick up the mess that his father had left behind at the tender age of fifteen.He had left behind everything he had held dear at eighteen, obtaining passage on a French vessel as a cabin boy. He had lived on the ship for two years, when one day he had been approached by some wealthy Frenchmen.He had been drinking heavily, and with a few questions, had spilled his story, all of his hatred for the country of his birth, because he believed that it had taken his father away from him. They had scoffed when he had told the that he was a titled Lord, so he had shown them the papers his father had left behind, along with the seal of his rank, kept safely in a pouch he always carried with him.They had taken notice of him then, and had said that they would contact him the next day. He had not known then that he would become a spy for France, returning to England to claim his title, living on funds supplied to him in abundance for services rendered to an enemy country.But he adapted well to his lifestyle as a traitor, though he didn't think of himself in that light.He was just paying England back for orphaning him.The killing fascinated him the most. Taking the lives of people when they did not even suspect him, walking among them unnoticed, considered incapable of such a heinous deed, gave him a feeling of power he never expected. Stealing information from the bungling fools that called themselves Lords, when drinking them under the table, or losing bets while gambling with them, it helped him achieve his objectives nicely. When he had met James, an up-and-coming spy for the W.O., in the dim alleyways of France while the bastard was chasing le tueur, his longtime friend and confidant, he had seen his chance to kill the man who had evaded him for so long.But when he had removed the dagger from its sheath and prepared to kill his opponent, James had not stayed quiet. In the fight that had ensued, he had managed only to scar James face, while escaping with a broken rib when he had seen Conrad approaching them . He had been thankful for the dark, and the long cloth that covered all of his face except his eyes, making it impossible for the men to recognize him.His friend had died that day, killed by the Englishmen, and he had sworn revenge on James and his partner. But the thought that haunted him was whether le tueur had said anything about him as he took his last breaths. He wanted to think his friend would not do something like that, and the W.O. didn't seem to be looking for him. But one could never be too sure of such things.This travelling between England and France was tiring sometimes. He wondered how it would be to live like a normal person. A life without murder and mayhem. It was not for him, that was a fact.He sighed. But one thing was for sure, if James married the chit as he was supposed to, it would make his plan for revenge much, much simpler. He smiled.And much more exciting.

Chapter 16

For the second time that day, Olivia woke up in unfamiliar surroundings. But this time she was not as disoriented as she had been before.Olivia had a faint recollection of being carried from the carriage by James as they reached his country home, him dismissing the servants till the next day when introductions would be made. She had been carried up the stairs to this room, The Master Suite if the décor was any indication, she thought.Almost everything in the room was burgundy, be it the drapes or the carpet. The previous Earl must have slept alone, she mused, for there was not even a slight touch of feminity. This made her realize that she did not know anything about James's mother. She must ask him sometime.By the colour of the sky visible because of the drawn drapes, she believed it was almost nighttime. The shock of the day had helped her to sleep like a babe. She did not like being weak, and a fit of the vapors was definitely a weakness.Suddenly she was aware of someone else in the room. Turning, she saw James sitting in a chair pulled up to her bedside. His gaze was hooded as he watched her quietly. All at once she felt self conscious. What was one supposed to say in such situations, when your husband-to-be sat at your bedside after saving you from a disastrous scandal?"How are you feeling Olivia?", James asked, after contemplating her sleepily rumpled form for far longer than necessary. This need, this longing, for her was ridiculous! He had to get himself under control! It would not do for him to let his guard down. Not till the traitor was found.Holding a limp Olivia in his arms had reminded him of the need to keep her safe. The thought of her used for revenge against him made him feel cold throughout his body. She had slept for three hours, her breathing deep and even. She even slept seductively, he thought. Or maybe it was just him."I- I am feeling well, my L-Lord."What was wrong with her? Stop behaving like a simple-minded ninny and show some courage Olivia, she reprimanded herself. He was just a man!An absolutely ravishing specimen of one, a tiny voice in her head reminded her slyly, causing her to slap her hands to her cheeks to contain the blush that blossomed on her face at her own thoughts.James looked at her trying to hide her flaming cheeks, and his voice turned teasing as he asked, "A touch of fever, then, m'dear? Perhaps we should summon the physician?"She turned a murderous glare on him as she said, "You know very well there is no fever James! As you should, what with you kissing my brow every few minutes to ascertain that there was none!"James felt heat creep up his neck as he was reminded of his behavior. But he had thought she wouldn't notice since she was sleeping. His joke had backfired miserably."Well?", asked Olivia, her confidence returning at the sight of his embarrassed face. But she had to admit that it did not make him any less breathtaking. If anything, he looked even more handsome!Unbidden a thought entered her head.They were not married yet! And she was in his bed!"Olivia, it is alright. Tomorrow we shall get married by special license and you shall be my wife in every sense. Sleeping in my bed does not defy propriety. Well at least not too much. Stop agitating yourself over something of no consequence."As the calm tone of James voice reached her ears, she closed her eyes, mortified that she had spoken those thoughts aloud. But something he had said registered in her mind."How did you acquire a special license at such short notice?", she asked, curious to know the answer."I, well- I had it made the day I had come to apologize to you.", James said in a rush.Her eyes softened as she looked at him."I realized that I wanted to marry you that day. So I got it made as soon as possible. I had been carrying it around with me since. Which is why I had felt..... afraid that I would lose you, when I realized Townsend had abducted you. I wanted to wring his neck for taking you away. I-", James stopped as he felt her hand stroke his cheek.Looking up and noticing her warm green gaze, he pulled her onto his lap, wrapping his hands around her waist."Shh....", she said, settling her head comfortably on his shoulder as he continued to hold her like she would vanish if he let go. "I'm here.""Olivia? Did you hear what I said?"James voice snapped her out of her reverie.There she went romanticizing her life again. Of course he wouldn't spit out all of his feelings yet! They weren't even married! But no, her mind had to go and show her things that were currently impossible. He did want to marry her, but even she knew that men married for desire and not love. There were exceptions to that as well, like men who married for a lady's dowry, or seldom, even for love.But she would be fooling herself to think that theirs would turn out to be a love match. What with James being so secretive and hardly showing all his emotions, and she being an outspoken and stubborn person, it seemed to her to be a difficult proposition.But she still wished to marry him. Despite all the odds. What was wrong with her mind and heart, she did not wish to examine too closely. Because she believed that what she would find there, could only cause her heartbreak. And it was a weakness. One she did not wish to leave open to the world, most especially James.So she smiled at him politely, saying,"Yes my Lord, you said that you had the license made the day you came to apologize to me. But shan't we have a small ceremony after wards ? Or a feast for the townspeople perhaps? "James looked at her, wondering what had brought the sad look to her eyes only moments before, which she had quickly replaced with an overbright smile that had almost blinded him with its intensity. Now she was asking him if they could hold a gathering! In his haste, he hadn't asked her if she would like to invite her parents tomorrow, even though they were to be wed by special license. In fact, he hadn't thought about her needs at all, and the realization made him feel like a cad.But before he could ask her about it, she began chattering about how nice it would be to meet the tenants who likely wouldn't have had much excitement in their lives of late, and how much it would help to lift their spirits.Seeing her so concerned about the tenants, made him realize yet again how lucky he was.He made a mental note to send a footman with a message inviting Olivia's parents and brother to

Bentham Park. He did not deserve the beauty in front of him, who hadn't thought about herself even once even though she had just had a stressful day,which would have made a normal Lady take to her bed for at least two days, what with being abducted from her own doorstep. At this thought, he had to take a few deep breaths to clear the red haze that had appeared in front of his vision.Townsend was still wet behind the ears, foolish notions clouding his brain. He had blanched when Olivia had left them alone together, apologizing profusely to James, insisting that he would never have pursued Olivia if he had any knowledge of James's intentions. James had let him go with a warning to never abduct a Lady without her consent in the matter, which was laughable in itself, but the Viscount had been to terrified to take notice."My dear, that is a splendid idea! I shall organize a get together for the afternoon. All our tenants will be invited. " ,he said, giving her a comforting smile."I appreciate you considering my suggestion, my Lord."Olivia was relieved. He would be a just husband if not a loving one."Meanwhile, I have a surprise for you in the adjoining room. You may tell me if you need anything else. Our marriage shall take place in the morning at ten o'clock. Is that alright?", James said, thinking of the 'surprise' he had for her.He felt uncomfortably like he was approaching their marriage as if it was a business investment, but was at a loss at how to express himself. Remarkably, she was the one person who had the power to befuddle him like no other. His tongue tied itself into knots around her, but he'd be damned if he'd let anyone know his weakness was his wife!Her next words threw him completely off track. Befuddle him, indeed!"Well, a Lady likes to be proposed to", she said, though his expression made her regret her words almost immediately. But the flustered expression on his face (which she knew he would object to if she told him) disappeared as quickly as it had come. And his next actions made her think, there might be hope after all.James saw the regret on her face at his shocked expression (it was NOT embarrassment!) and was instantly contrite. Why did he keep making these blunders when it came to her, his Siren? And as for her earlier request............James dropped down onto one knee, reaching into his pocket to retrieve the ring he had had made for his wife-to-be, and said, "Olivia Mabel Wynter, will you do me the great honour of becoming my wife?"Olivia looked into the eyes that had intrigued her since she had seen them for the first time, and seeing the sincerity, and what she fancied to be love in them, uttered a simple, "Yes", before placing her hand in his outstretched one as he slipped the plain gold band on her finger.Standing up, James gave her a chaste kiss on her cheek, at which she blushed and remembering something reached for the chain on her neck. Unfastening the clasp, she slid an identical gold band off the chain.Smiling at the stupefied look on James face, she herself picked up his hand and mimicked his earlier actions, blushing slightly at her own forwardness.James was overwhelmed at her gesture. Looking at the ring in wonder, he wondered how much more she would surprise him in the years to come. One thing was for certain, he would never tire of the mystery that was Olivia Wynter.

Chapter 17

Olivia stared at her reflection in the mirror and wondered how her life had changed since yesterday. She was now a countess. The Countess of Winchester, James wife! The woman in the mirror was not so different than what she was used to seeing everyday. But nonetheless, everything had changed.Last night, when she had entered her room on James insistence, she had been pleasantly surprised to see the entire array of gowns in every colour imaginable that filled her wardrobe to bursting. The sizes were perfect, leading her to wonder how he had the dresses made with such haste, that fit her to perfection.Out of all the gowns however, one had caught her eye in particular. It was a pure light grey in colour, and matched James eyes perfectly. She went over to it, fingering the material that looked so fragile as to crumble at the lightest touch of her fingers. It shimmered like the wings of an angel. She would wear it tomorrow morning, she decided. It was perfect."Personally I like this one."J ames voice, husky with an emotion she could not place, made her turn towards him. He stood a few feet away, and looking at the gown in his hands, she felt the tenderness for him grow.It was the exact shade of her own eyes, even the bodice had embroidery in gold that resembled the golden flecks in them. The green silk skirt looked like it was made from tiny emeralds, flashing with fire."It is beautiful, James. But I shall always love this one better.", she said, clutching the grey gown to her breast like it might vanish if she let go."We must agree to disagree then, dearest. But both gowns will complement you nicely, I think.", James replied, smiling now.They had retired then, after having a light dinner, and Olivia had lain awake till midnight, wondering what the next day would bring.She remembered how her parents and Oliver had surprised her that morning, appearing at Bentham Park for the ceremony. When she had asked them they had said that it was James who had sent a messenger the previous evening inviting them to their wedding, such as it was. When she had stolen a glance at her fiancé, she had caught him looking at her with a hooded expression, which she had returned with a grateful smile. Because after seeing her family again, she had realized just how much she needed them with her at this moment. And how much she would miss them later.The ceremony had been small, and after signing the papers and saying their vows, and her mother crying when James slipped the ring on her finger and placed a chaste kiss on her forehead, they had had a sumptuous breakfast. Her father had gone with James to the study then, to discuss the terms of her dowry, no doubt. One more thing she despised about Society. But her father would not budge on that point, even though he had been tolerant of most of her opinions. 'Matter of honour', he had said, and ended the subject."Olivia, are you happy with this?", Oliver, who had been silent for the most part of the morning now spoke up. She understood his unspoken words 'with this marriage'."Far too late to be asking me this, now isn't it brother?""Olivia, I swear if you make a joke of this....""What could you possibly do Olly?"His face turned red at the hated nickname. But before he could reply, their mother stepped in."Olivia dear, do not tease your brother. I know that this union has your father's blessing, but it would ease our minds a great deal if you were to say it with your own mouth." Her mother's words wiped the smile of her face, and it was a serious faced Olivia that replied."Yes, mother, Oliver, I am happy. The Earl is all I could want in a husband and we shall manage nicely."Why her words sounded dry and emotionless to her own ears, she would not think about. But her mother and brother seemed not to notice, as they both smiled at her and resumed their conversation.After breakfast however, Oliver went to take a stroll of the gardens and stables adjoining the house. As her father and James had yet to emerge from the study, that left Olivia and her mother alone, and her mother expressed her wish to speak privately with Olivia, who led the way to her room."My what a beautiful room!", the duchess exclaimed, eyeing the pale pink walls and large bed appreciatively. The previous occupant had had the room furnished exquisitely, the furniture of the highest quality, the carpet soft and plush, and the watercolour that hung opposite the bed was a calming scene depicting wildflowers that looked as if their scent might reach you any moment."It really is. What is it you wanted to speak to me about, mama?""Well I-that is to say I- You do remember the talk we had after your first season, don't you dear?"Her mother looked at her questioningly, a slight blush staining her pale complexion. Sudden realization dawned in Olivia's mind as she recalled the time when her mother had told her about what happened between a man and his wife. Blinking a little at her mother's awkwardness she reassured her."Yes I do remember, mama. You do not need to repeat that conversation!"Because if she had to endure that once again, she might just die of embarrassment!"That's done then.", her mother sighed with relief, "But you shall take care wont you Livvy? Men are such fickle creatures sometimes, you see. They want us to be soft and strong at the same time, which makes it difficult to live with them sometimes. But now he is your protection and whatever right or wrong you do reflects on him. So you should not give the Earl undue grief because of your antics, do you understand? In time you shall grow comfortable in each others company, and disagreements shall be few and far in between. But till then you must tread carefully where his feelings and ego are concerned. Just until the tenuous thread by which your marriage hangs, strengthens, you must be strong. Be happy, my dear girl."By the time her mother said those last words, both of them had their eyes brimming over. Olivia went to her mother and rested her head on her lap, her mother stroking her hair. They stayed like that for some more time before a servant requested them to come downstairs, as the Duke's carriage had been prepared to leave for London.Downstairs, Oliver had give her a bone-crushing hug and whispered in her ear, "If you ever need me to beat up His Lordship, I shall be happy to oblige.", making her want to cry.Her father was more subtle in his emotions, kissing her cheek and saying, "Goodbye, my Olive."She smiled at the nickname he had called her since she was little, and, teary-eyed, looked at her mother, who wiped her daughter's eyes. "Now, now, no more of that, Livvy. You shall visit us in a month or so, shan't you? I wish you all the happiness in the world, both of you."Surprising James, she went and kissed his cheek. "Take care of my daughter, my Lord. You shall require some patience, but I am sure if anyone can manage it, you can." She said to him, and at Olivia's outraged, "Mama!", she accepted her husband's hand laughing at Olivia's face, and went down the steps and into the carriage, followed by both the men, and soon the carriage was out of sight.She had then gone up to her room to change into the green dress that James had held up yesterday. The picnic lunch James had organized was to be held in the vast expanse of the Bentham Park grounds, and all the villagers and tenants were to attend.Now she stood in front of the mirror in the green gown, as she wondered what her life had in store for her next. Perhaps at the luncheon, she would have some fun. But she must hurry downstairs for that, James would appreciate her being punctual.So she did.

Chapter 18

"Take care of my daughter, my Lord"The words had been echoing in James head since the morning, when Olivia's mother had kissed him on the cheek (Kissed him! He still couldn't believe it!) and said those words. They had reminded him of the traitor, and the fact that he had not been caught yet.Every moment that the traitor was out in the open was enough to increase the danger to Olivia's well-being. And it was all his fault. Unbidden, the image of his mother's pale, lifeless body entered his mind. No, he would not have another death on his conscience. The Lord knew, his soul couldn't take it.Trying to conquer the sadness creeping into his heart at just the thought of life without Olivia, he recalled her holding the grey dress the previous evening. The dressmaker had assured him that his Lady would love the gown more than any other. Confused at her statement, he had asked her why."Because it matches your eyes, my Lord.", she had replied, her round face red with joy at his obvious embarrassment at her answer. Even then he had not believed the woman.But Olivia's face while looking at the gown had dispelled his misconception. It had shone with something akin to happiness, and he had been assailed once more by his never-ending desire for her. His voice had been husky when he had shown her the gown that he had had made specifically imagining her eyes, that day when he had made her angry while they waltzed, by innocently saying that young ladies only read ton gossip and fashion plates.Getting the dresses finished in time to give them to her as a wedding gift had cost him a pretty penny, but seeing her today in the gown whose colour matched his eyes, her own shining with hope and belief in him, it had been repaid a thousandfold.He fingered the ring she had given him, and wondered once again when she would cease to surprise him. It was time to go for the picnic lunch on the grounds. The preparations had been flawless and he had kept track of every aspect of the party, ascertaining that it would be nice enough for the villagers. He knew the importance of the tenants in his life, and also that neglecting them was counter productive. This gathering would be a test of Olivia's abilities to act as a host, and interact with the tenants, he knew, and he had absolute confidence in her. He knew that with her charming smile and confidence, she would win over the gruffest of the village elders. The thought made him smile.Just as he approached the main staircase , Olivia stumbled to a halt a the top. Would she never cease to entice him? His Siren, garbed in the gown that had been his favorite from the start, smiled tremulously at him from her position atop the long column of stairs. He wondered what was the cause for that.But before he could think any further, she swiftly gathered her skirts and resting her bottom on the stair rail, slid down the staircase. By the time she reached the end James had regained his wits and rushed up, catching her before she slammed into the banister. Hoisting her into his arms, he stared at her incredulously ."What is wrong with you?"Her answer was to burst into laughter."Oh - my- God! That-was-amazing..... And-your face!", she choked out between her laughter."Olivia", James growled,"Why did you do that?""To see how you would react, of course! And it was priceless! I am sorry if I caused you any distress, my Lord.", she said, still giggling."You, my dear, are a baggage! And I know just how to punish you." James words caused Olivia's laughter to subside. Punish? James didn't seem like the type of man who would beat a woman, but who was she to say? She hardly knew him and-Before she could think of anything more worse, James slung her over his shoulder like a sack of onions, with nary a grunt nor groan. It was like she was as light as a feather."James! Put me down! Oh dear, what will the servants think! James John Richardson! Let me down this instant!"But James paid her no heed, as he carried her out the door, passing an astonished Pemberly, and climbed into the waiting phaeton, where he dropped her ungracefully in the seat, plopping down next to her."James, why in heavens name did you do that? Do you even realize what the servants-" her protest was cut off almost immediately."If you were so concerned about what the servants would think madam, then you would not have pulled something like that stunt on the staircase! Carrying you over my shoulder was just my way to teach you to think of the consequences before you do something you would regret later. What if you had fallenand broken your fool neck? What then?" James stared straight ahead, images of her deathly pale skin taunting him."I am skilled at the 'stunt' I was 'pulling', my Lord." She said primly. "Oliver and I have practiced since we were little, and I know when exactly to jump off the rail, and how to position my feet to absorb the impact of swiftly getting down. I also know-""I forbid you to repeat your actions hereafter, Olivia. A countess must live upto the expectations of her peers. None of this dilly-dallying is appropriate. You shall behave with propriety and grace as my wife. I hope I shall not have to repeat this." His words stunned Olivia into absolute silence. Though she did not say anything to him, her thoughts were in a whirl.How dare he say such a thing to her? Propriety and grace? Was she to be treated like a china-doll then, who always smiled and was perfectly groomed, but was brittle? She did not believe that her actions mediated such a harsh reprimand! But if that was what he wished, she would not disappoint him.***What had gotten into him? James thought. He had never meant to sound like all the controlling husbands of the ton rolled into one! But what had come out of his mouth when she had systematically started to explain how well she knew how to slide down a stair rail, had made him sound like one. And he knew she was incensed. She hadn't said anything so far, but he knew that her temper boiled just under the surface. She was his passionate Siren after all.He would have to think about how he would make it up to her. Before she actually took his ill-advice to heart.

Chapter 19

James alighted from the phaeton swiftly, turning around and holding out his hands for Olivia to take. Their ride had been silent and mostly consisting of a frosty countenance on Olivia's part, and he was now worried about what he would have to do to make her forgive him.

Kissing her was the first thing that came to mind, but he quickly erased that thought from his mind, albeit with some difficulty. He was sure that she would not be amenable to that idea, since a proper countess of the ton (he winced at his own words) would never indulge in such a public display of affection, even with her husband.

Cursing himself for a fool, James decided that he could start by giving her an upper hand with the villagers.

When she descended from the phaeton - descended was the only way to describe it, as she held her head high and trod softly, with nary a hair out of place, features cool and composed like a queen, James thought- and took his proffered hand, they walked towards the crowd of people standing in a circle.

The women were either round and red-faced or thin and graceful. The older men had gruff features, the years of hard work taking a toll on how often they smiled. The younger men were more jolly, flirting with the young maidens, who blushed prettily. The children had been told to stand still in a group to wait till the Lord an' his new Lady wife bid them otherwise. Still, pigtails were being pulled and bodies pushed, suppressed excitement making the tiny people restless.

It was this restlessness that first caught Olivia's attention. The second was the old couple approaching them, the woman was smiling widely in her plump face, while her husband's hand was around her shoulders, though he wasn't smiling.

"Welcome back, my Lord, and our best wishes on your marriage.", the man was the first to speak, and Olivia was surprised to see a hint of pride in his gaze. He was proud of James? The thought gave Olivia pause. But before she could think further, James himself spoke.

"You know that you needn't refer to me that way, sir."

"You will always be our Jamie, son. But here, in front of so many of your tenants-"

"That is inconsequential. Please, don't argue on this point, sir, I beseech you. You are like my father in all ways except by blood. Call me James."

The man sighed."Alright, James."

"Don't remember me, do ye now, lad? All grown up are we, the womenfolk to small to take notice of now?"

James turned a bemused gaze to Margaret, or Maggie as he had called her when she had been his nursemaid so many years before.

"How could I forget you Ma'am? After all that ear pinching you did, you were permanently imprinted on my brain, or should I say my poor ears?" So saying, James leaned in and kissed her cheek, making the old woman shoo him with her hands, her eyes sparkling with an emotion akin to a mother's love.

"Off with you, lad! You deserve every pinch I gave your 'poor' ears! A terror is what you were, and how your mother fretted for you, only I know!" At the sudden rigidity in James posture, however, the woman changed the subject quickly, latching on to a more pressing matter.

"Are you going to introduce your wife to us laddie? The poor thing is standing there looking so lost! Forgotten our manners already, then?", she said, giving him a disapproving look. James caught on quickly, and he placed his hand on Olivia's waist.

"This is my wife, Lady Olivia Richardson, Countess of Winchester. Olivia, this is Brian and Margaret Willoughby.", James said, waiting to see her reaction. Would she be cold or would she-

"It is a pleasure to meet you both. It is obvious that James respects and loves you very much, and I'm glad for that." When the couple in front of them smiled and politely greeted her as well, Olivia asked Margaret, "But I must ask, why are the poor children standing there so uncomfortably? Surely they must be allowed to run about and play!"

The old woman told her that they had been told to stand still for their arrival, making Olivia chuckle.

"Oh dear. Then I must free them, mustn't I ?"

She walked toward the group of children, whose faces were solemn and eyes downcast as she came to stand before them. All but one little girl, whose blue eyes and light brown hair shone as she came up to Olivia, pulling her skirt as she asked,

"Are you the pretty Lady who me mam told me to wait for? Can we play now, mam? I have a new dolly and I want to show her to Annie! Can we please play-"

Suddenly a woman who looked just like the girl, except that she had warm brown eyes, rushed up to them, apologizing profusely.

" I am sorry for the child's rudeness, my Lady. It shall not happen again. Livvy, apologize to her Ladyship! The children have been standing for sometime, you see, my Lady, so they are just – Oh I didn't mean to say they were standing because you were late! I just-"

"It is alright, miss, you needn't be so scared! I understand that the children would hate this inactivity." Olivia tried to placate the harried woman, now kneeling to look straight into the little girl's eyes.

"Hello dear. You were correct. I am the Lady your mother told you about. My name is Olivia. Is that your name as well?" Olivia said, recalling the mother calling her 'Livvy'. The child blinked once, as if surprised that she was being spoken to, then spoke in a happy voice.

"My name is Olivia too! You are really pretty, mam, just like me mam said." Olivia couldn't stop the smile that bloomed on her face at the child's words. Cupping her cheek, she spoke to her in a solemn tone.

"Thank you, Livvy. You are a pretty girl as well. And now you can go and show your new dolly to Annie. Go on, all of you! You can go to play! But wash your hands in the stream before lunch! Now go, shoo!"

Her words had an immediate effect. All the children cheered, and still screaming they ran away to play with each other. Olivia stood up, intending to speak to Olivia's mother. The poor woman seemed so upset!

But as soon as she turned around, she found her gaze being held captive by her Pirate's grey eyes, and Olivia wondered how long it would take her to get used to their piercing intensity. Unknowingly, she found herself staring at him, mesmerized despite her anger about their earlier conversation. The words that came from his lips were like music to her ears.

"When will you cease to surprise me? Here I am, thinking that you will behave in a particular way, but you do the complete opposite! I am constantly amazed by you. You are a wonder, Olivia, and not to mention 'pretty', but I would prefer to call you beautiful." At the violent blush that spread over her cheeks, he brushed a curl at her forehead, murmuring softly, "My wife. I do not know what I have done to make myself worthy enough to call you so, but I am grateful for it. Please ignore anything that I said to you earlier. You-" He was cut off, surprisingly, by Olivia, who put a finger to his lips, her eyes shining.

"Hush. I understand." Suddenly mischief glinted in her eyes, and she continued, " But I must agree that you are indeed lucky to have me as your wife. I say this with all modesty, of course. I am a countess after all. And we all know that I am the soul of propriety and-" She stopped her monologue, noticing the light of battle in James eyes, that clearly told her that she would have a repeat performance of that morning if she did not cease that instant. Timidly, she looked at his raised eyebrow, not uttering a word.

"I hate to repeat myself, but you my dear are a prime baggage! Now let us go to the villagers, we must begin the round of dances that has been scheduled before lunch is served." James led her towards the group of people who stood close by, still a bit startled by the previous occurrences, but looking forward to the dancing and merriment ahead.

There was a round of applause as they took to the 'floor'- a space cleared for the dancing, and were soon surrounded by couples dancing to the country dance music that played. The music for the dances was fast paced, and Olivia found herself tired and hungry after it was all over. She had danced with so many men, some old, some younger than herself, and occasionally going back into James arms for a few minutes. She had enjoyed every moment of it.

And now James was leading her to the shade of a nearby tree, after they had collected their picnic basket like everyone else. But James stopped in his tracks suddenly.

"Olivia, wait here for a moment. I left the blanket in the phaeton, I'll go fetch it. Don't try to haul the basket to the tree by yourself, do you hear me? Just stay put." So saying, he turned around and walked towards the phaeton that stood some distance away from the entire party.

Olivia sighed. Her Pirate would know exactly what she was going to do as soon as he left! But she saw no point in provoking his anger again, so she turned to look in the opposite direction where a stand of trees could be seen clearly.

But there she saw a lone horseman, a hunting cap on his head staring in her direction.

What could he be doing over- But she couldn't complete her thought.

BANG

She looked down just in time to see the red stain quickly staining her side.

And James favourite gown...........

Chapter 20

*BANG*The sound of the pistol being fired had turned James heart to ice.Turning around, he saw Olivia, his Olivia, looking at something on her abdomen. He did not know what she saw there, but in the next second, she crumpled to the grass.And he ran.He didn't reach quickly enough to catch her, of course, but the fall was the least of her troubles. James felt the anger and despair rise in him quickly at the sight of the bullet wound in her side. Quickly he ripped the blanket he had in half, and pressed the cloth to staunch the blood flow Dropping to the ground, he pulled her head onto his lap, murmuring soothing words to her pale form, his own skin turning pasty with worry.Already the villagers had reached them, and James bellowed for the village physician, who appeared quickly, and assessing the scene before him, knelt to observe Olivia's wound."It is a flesh wound, my Lord. She has lost some blood, but a few days of rest, sutures, and some laudanum, and her Ladyship should be right as rain. We should take her to Bentham now, where I will clean and dress the wound."With that, the physician stood up, and when James picked up Olivia's limp body, began to walk towards his own horse whose saddle-bags had his emergency supplies.Brian Willoughby came up to James and said in a quiet voice, "James, three of the villagers have followed the horseman who... did this. Whatever news they have, I shall send them to you. Also, I wish to speak to you about your behavior right now. You acted like you were not surprised at-""Sir, I shall speak to you in the evening at Bentham. At this moment, taking care of my wife is my first priority. Please bring along your wife as well. We shall speak after dinner." James said in a clipped voice, the irritation at his own inability to go and hunt the bastard who had hurt his Siren coming out clearly in his tone. The old man must have recognized this and so he nodded politely and stepped back to let James pass on to the phaeton.As the vehicle rolled onwards, James held Olivia close to him, his body reeling with the realization of how close he had come to losing her. He couldn't go to search for the rider till he was assured that she was safe and sound. Hopefully the men who had gone after the scoundrel would catch him so he could know his identity. Though he had a sinking suspicion that it was the traitor, or at least someone sent by him.Carrying her up the stairs to their room, he entered to see the physician already waiting and a maid placing a basin of warm water on the nightstand. He went a softly laid her on the bed.The doctor worked quickly and efficiently, though James grimaced as he cut out a patch of the fabric covering the wound and Olivia moaned softly. Even the thought of her in pain was unbearable to James. Still he forced himself to look at the wound marring her delicate skin. It would probably be his only glimpse of it until the traitor was caught.During the ride back to Bentham, James had taken a decision. Since the traitor had attacked Olivia since she was close to him, he had to stay away from her. Also he must spread the rumour that they were an unhappy couple, so he would stay away from Olivia and come for James himself. This meant staying away in all respects. So they would have no wedding night.After the doctor had bandaged Olivia's side and left after prescribing the amount of laudanum and rest she would require, James sent for two maids to take care of her when she woke up, and going to her side, he placed a kiss on her brow, murmuring softly, "No one will dare to hurt you again, Olivia. Not while you are in my care. I shall take care of it now. You must understand that I have to keep some distance from you now so you are not targeted again. It will cost me dearly, but I shall do it. Rest, and get well soon, it breaks my heart to see you thus. Goodbye, my dear."And he walked from the room, leaving his sleeping wife behind.***Her head hurt.That was the first thought that popped into Olivia's mind as she groaned, feeling the dull thudding increase to a pounding rhythm as she tried to sit up in the bed.The bed?How was she in a bed? Wasn't she supposed to be at the picnic? Where was James?Suddenly the memory of the horseman invaded her senses, causing a dizzy panic to spread through her system, and she threw off the bedcovers to stare uncomprehendingly at the bandage covering her side that was visible through her torn gown. Looking at the cut fabric, she almost fainted again. That wonderful gown! Oh dear Lord!Suddenly her shoulders were steadied and pillows were arranged behind her back so she could sit up properly. Looking up, she found herself faced by two maids, both with smiling faces."How do you feel, my Lady?""Does your head ache, my Lady?""Are you comfortable, my Lady?""Would you like something to eat, my Lady?""Can I-""Stop! The both of you! How many questions am I supposed to answer at once?" Olivia said ending the maids concerned enquiries in an instant, pressing her fingers to the throbbing in her head, she spoke quietly."I am feeling fine, I just have a bit of a headache. As for comfort, I shall feel that only when I am allowed to speak to my husband about what happened. And also, I don't wish to eat anything, thank you. Now if you would go fetch my husband?"Olivia said, wondering why James had not been there beside her when she woke up. How long had it been since the shot?When both the girls seemed reluctant to move, she asked them why they were not moving."My Lady, it is- we mean to say-""What is it? Speak up, now!""His Lordship is not at home at this moment. He has gone to take care of something important, so he had stationed us here to take care of you, my Lady.", came the reply, slightly muffled as the two stared at their feet while speaking.Olivia rubbed her chilled arms as a wave of sadness rolled over her. 'Something important'? So important that even she was secondary to it? And to think that she had thought they could come to love each other! He didn't even care for her wellbeing. Closing her eyes, she took a deep breath and put on a patently fake smile for the two young maids."I would like to change out of this gown into a robe. Both of you can help me, it is going to be slightly cumbersome. Afterwards, you could pour me some laudanum, I am sure the doctor has prescribed it."At their mute

nods, Olivia sent them to fetch the robe and the medicine. Lying back down on the bed, she thought of the lone rider, and why anyone would want to kill her, for there was no doubt in her mind that the rider had come to kill her.And why her husband had left her alone, when the thing she wanted most was to be held by him.**************
**Meanwhile James was at the picnic spot, speaking with the three men who, even after trying their best, had failed to outrun the shooter's horse to intercept him.Simon, who appeared to be the most verbal out of the three, had just finished narrating their tale to James.How they had heard the shot, and quickly noticing the shooter had sprinted to their mounts, speeding after the man, who had a proper head start, and apparently a prime piece of horseflesh."Like bloody lightening 'e was, though Will 'ere almost caught 'im once. But in the end we lost his tracks at the road leading to London. There be a horde of carriages belonging to the fancy, creating enough dust to obscure your vision for a mile, me Lord. Pardon us for not catching the bastard, sir. If it weren't for them carriages, we would 'ave 'im on a pike for ye."James tried to suppress the anger that insisted on blistering their ears for letting the man go. It wasn't their fault. Now everything was in his hands. He would have to contact Connie tonight. Having him here to guard Olivia would ease his mind a great deal. That way he wouldn't have to be around her tempting presence every minute of the day.But from the men's report, the rider had been standing quite far away. He would have had to be a good marksman to have even hit his target anywhere from such a distance. No doubt he had aimed to kill. But

the distance had been too great for an accurate shot. Thank The Lord for that bit of luck!He let the men go along, with a message for the Willoughbys that he would meet them tomorrow. Mounting Sultan, he rode to the spot where the rider had shot Olivia from. And prepared to search for clues leading him to the man who tried to kill his wife.All the while wondering what Olivia would think if she woke up without him next to her.Would she feel hurt? Or happy?The second possibilty angered him so much that he spurred Sultan to go faster, completely forgetting the purpose of the ride for a few moments, letting the wind tousle his hair into disarray, telling the rational side of his brain, which insisted on speaking to Olivia and getting the matter clarified before jumping to conclusions, to go to hell, before he stopped and rode back the way he had come, trying to get his mind under control.This time he kept his thoughts focused on the shooter.

Traitor 2

Sweat. Cheap whisky. Whores.It was the stench that permeated the alley walls, as the lone man scurried along the darkened and dirty pathway.Dirty Pete was his name, and to the uppity members of the ton, he was part of the lowest rung on the ladder. A hired marksman. A thug.A thug who was in deep waters. With no boat in sight.He had been so confident in his abilities, and had not wasted any time in sealing the deal with that fancy gentleman that had approached him the day before about a mark.He had been at one of the seedier bars that saw hide nor hair of any kind of gentry, so when the man had approached him and he had noticed the pristine clothes the man wore, he had smelled easy money. It was a known fact in the criminal class that the gentry were easy targets to obtain money. They had plenty of it, and lacked the brains to regulate how much they spent.But this man had been cleverer than Pete had anticipated. And now he was on the run, because though he didn't realize at the time, he had sold his soul to the devil.And the devil wanted his payment.Rounding a corner, he plastered his body to the wall, cautious of the slightest sound. How could he have bungled the whole thing up so much?Killing the woman should have been so easy. But he hadn't thought about any kind of picnic and that there would be such a crowd. And the long distance shooting he would have to do to get the wench.Everything had turned against him that morning, and seeing those three men chase after him, he had bolted like a hare, the horse that the gentleman had provided helping him outrun them, but he now had bigger problems.He would try to catch the first ship out of London at dawn. He just had to get to his lodgings to collect whatever savings he had, and he would leave with the clothes on his back, find some shelter for the remaining hours till dawn and he would be safe.Just an alley away from his shack, however, he felt a chill go down his spine. Something had changed in the air, and it was making the hair on the back of his neck stand up. Suddenly, a figure stepped out of the fog, and a cold voice spoke quietly."Where do you think you are going, Pete?"It was enough for him to start begging for his life. He fell to his knees and groveled before the terrifying spectacle before him, but when the man took out a pistol, he knew he was going to die that night.But by God, he'd go down fighting.Quickly he took his own pistol out of his inner coat pocket.But before he could aim at his assailant, saw the blood gush out of his own heart and stain his ripped coat red.Falling to the ground, his last thought was, God help the woman he's after.***** ***As he watched Dirty Pete take his last breaths, he thought, that is why you never send someone else to do your job. Especially an inept person.It had sounded so simple. Pete had killed enough people successfully to give him the job to kill the new countess. But the incompetent fool had spoiled everything! All his carefully laid out plans were now ruined!But he would not panic. Hadn't he done the right thing already? Killed ol' Dirty Pete before he could ruin anyone else's plans. Yes, he had done the right thing.Leaving the body behind, he walked for a few minutes before he reached the shack where he had tethered his horse. No one knew about it, and even the thieves did not venture so far astray of the city.Mounting the stallion, he began the trip to his town lodgings, his mind plotting the course ahead. The girl had to go. She was the weak link, and no doubt the Earl would take her death as a hard blow. The way the sod had been behaving for the past weeks confirmed his suspicions that it was a love match to be certain.But now he would have to go to Shropshire himself. How tedious.Perhaps he could poison the chit? Servants were so easily bought. A few coins in the right pockets and you had them willing to do your bidding instantly.But that would be too easy. He must think of something complex.That way he had so much more excitement.In any case, the Earl and countess of Winchester would have a visit from him soon.Oh, Goody.

Chapter 21

Olivia opened her eyes gingerly, as the first rays of dawn hit her eyelids. She stretched as much as her throbbing body would allow her and pushed her matted hair behind her ears. She had been too tired to tie it up before she had dozed off last night. Pushing herself upright, she rested her head on the headboard, looking around her.And frowned at the armchair placed next to the bed.The armchair that most definitely had not been there last night. She sighed. It must have been one of the maids sent to 'look after' her. She thanked the Lord that she wasn't sleeping there still. It would be dreadful to watch a person sleep all night long. And she wouldn't like to trouble someone that way, servant or not. In any case, she was feeling just a bit of pain where the bullet had grazed her side, and she wasn't about to complain about it.And now that she was awake, she felt likegoing for a walk. Certainly it was safe to stroll this early in the morn? As it is she had to speak to James about the previous day's occurrences, and the reason for his absence afterwards. She needed all the fresh air she could get.She was wearing just her thin chemise, so she walked towards the chair where she had draped her robe last night, and put it on. Spying a coat on the armchair, she picked it up. It was the same one that James had worn to the picnic.Feeling like a thief somehow, she let the fabric envelop her. And felt his scent cocoon her. Feeling somewhat bolstered by this, she let herself out of her chamber quietly, heading down the stairs and out of a door that the housekeeper had mentioned yesterday when she had come around with her dinner tray.Closing the door softly, as it was located close to the servant's chambers, she turned to find herself in the stunning Rose garden of Bentham Park. And what a garden!A large number of roses in every colour imaginable showcased their beauty in artfully arranged formations, each bush pruned in such a way as not to hinder the observer's path through the garden. In the shining rays of dawn, each flower appeared as if sculpted by a master artist. Even the dewdrops on them sent the sunlight reflecting in so many directions, creating a rainbow that dazzled the eye.Suddenly a hummingbird flitted just in front of her face, and the spell was broken as Olivia let out a little squeak of surprise. Feeling foolish at her reaction, she laughed, the tinkling sound coming forth from her lips involuntarily.Wandering further, she wondered why she hadn't seen hide nor hair of her husband since the picnic. She could not believe he did not wish to see her. Cold he could be, but James was not callous, she knew.And her wedding night! There had been no reason to even call it that! Maybe he had wanted to let her rest, as she knew for certain she was in no position to perform any kind of 'wifely' duties, what with the bandage covering her side, and the slight throbbing where the stitches pulled her skin.But he could have at least said good night, or checked on her health! She felt like life kept reminding her that it didn't go according to her wishes, but did what it wished. Ugh! She should stop acting like such a depressed person, just the fact that she was alive even after yesterday was enough to be thankful for.Turning a corner, her ears were assailed by a steadily cursing voice. Turning, she walked in the direction the sound was coming from, her curiosity piqued.Peering around a rather large rose bush while wondering what the gardener was doing at this hour, her eyes were met with an unexpected sight. So unexpected, that she could not contain the feminine giggle that escaped her lips.James stood amidst a few scattered flowers, a dagger in one hand, possibly being used to cut the flowers, and staring angrily at the other hand, the finger of which was bleeding rather profusely due to what she assumed was a thorn prick. At her giggle, however, he looked up, his annoyed gaze fading into a concerned one at the sight of her up and about so early in the morning."Olivia, shouldn't you be resting? Are you in pain? The laudanum was just on the nightstand, did you not see it? You should have woken up the maid, I sent her to sleep late in the night, but it is their job to cater to your needs, you mustn't hesitate to-" James stopped in his monologue abruptly, trying in vain to recover his composure, which had fractured on seeing her standing there, pale as a ghost, looking like a tiny, fragile fairy in his large coat, giggling at him of all things. His mind going blank, he just stared at her, waiting for her to reprimand him for his ungentlemanly behavior last night.But all she did was walk towards him, never breaking eye-contact, except for tearing off a piece of the sash of her robe. But when she looked at his bloody finger, she took his hand in hers, carefully locating the thorn that had pricked him, and gingerly taking it out. Then she did something that James would never have imagined.Taking his finger to her lips, she put it in her mouth, licking the blood off. By now, just looking at her had aroused every one of his senses, but she seemed unmoved as he watched her steadily, trying to control his animalistic impulses that threatened to overwhelm his rational ones.She took his finger out of her mouth slowly, watching him from under her lashes. If only she knew what she did to him with that look, she'd be a mile away by now, he thought to himself, his entire being protesting at the thought of her leaving. Taking the strip of silk she had torn, she tied it around his finger firmly, before looking up at him to ask, "Is that alright?"No, it isn't alright dammit! He wanted to shout. How he yearned for this vixen, and how important was it to keep her safe! Once he caught that bastard...."My Lord?""Yes, Olivia, it is fine."But he just couldn't resist kissing her on the cheek, though he would have loved to kiss much more than her cheeks at that moment. Fate was indeed a cruel mistress.Olivia blushed slightly at his gesture, chastising herself for her immature behavior. They were man and wife for heavens sake! She should expect such intimacies and much more. This train of thought however, caused her blush to deepen.James looked at her red cheeks and wondered what she would do if he kissed her full on the lips right then. But before he could think further, her face turned into a grimace of pain and she clutched her side, keening softly. This time, however, he was quick enough to hold her before she fell."I am okay, James, a slight dizziness is all.", said Olivia, but James was having none of it. In one fluid motion, he lifted her up carefully, as if she was made of glass. Despite her mumbled protests, made while resting her head on his shoulder, he carried her into the house, going straight up to their bedchamber, and laid her on the bed.Fetching the laudanum himself, James poured the prescribed dose and held it to her lips."I do not wish to drink it, it makes me drowsy. I am not some fragile flower that needs to be tended every moment of the day. I can-" Her tirade was cut off as James made a sound of frustration, slamming the tiny glass on the nightstand, and pacing to the far window to stare out at the rising sun."Do you realize that you almost died yesterday!" Where would he be if she had? Probably downing his tenth bottle of whiskey. And she tells him she doesn't need to be tended? The hell with that!James words brought everything into sharp focus for Olivia. The tautness of his muscles, as if he was waiting for something to happen, his clenched jaw and the muscle twitching in it. And through this display of anger, the worry in his eyes. Why hadn't she noticed it before? Because you were to busy drowning in self pity, a voice in her head answered."James- I apologize for making you worry. It-" Again she was cut off mid-sentence as he turned away from the window, striding over to her and picking her up by her arms and shouting at her bewildered form."Olivia, it is my duty to worry about you! I am your husband! You are mine! Under my protection! And I failed to protect you on the first day of our marriage..... And now you tell me that you don't need to be cared for.... But you do need to be cared for... and cherished."With those words, he jerked her body flush to his and kissed her.Why did she always ignite all of his senses to the limit? A taste of her sweet lips always, always made him forget every sorrow and trouble in his life. What had been before she had come into his life, her charm and inner beauty lighting up the darkest corners in his heart. Was this... No, it couldn't be. He should just concentrate on the physical needs in between them. Anything else was too precious to even think of.Olivia, however, was trying to keep herself from crying out in anguish. A duty? Was that all she was to him? She was trying to decide if she was in love with him, and he thought of her as a duty? It was enough to make her scream.Just then he deepened the kiss, and all thoughts of sadness vanished from her mind, and she moaned softly, clutching him closer.All she knew was that she must try to keep some distance from her Pirate, or she might get singed by the flame.

Chapter 22

Olivia would never have thought that she could get tired of lying in bed. But she was more than tired. She was frustrated. She had been lying in bed for the entire morning, the two maids that had been sent to care for her fluttering around the room, fluffing pillows, tidying her dresser, asking her if she wanted anything to eat or drink, being told 'no', still bringing up a tray laden with food and juice as well as water, her losing her temper, them calling James, him sternly telling her to rest and eat up, her feigning sleep so they would go away, them not going away......... And the cycle continued.She was contemplating jumping out of the window (a few broken bones would be preferable to this coddling!), when she heard the thundering of a lone horse's hooves along the gravel path, and wondered who would be in such a hurry to reach Bentham. Probably a messenger, she mused, dismissing the thought.But a few minutes later, there was a knock on the door and the maid went and opened it.James entered, his eyes meeting hers, trying to see if she seemed better. He walked to her side swiftly, picking up her hand to kiss it."How do you feel now Olivia? Have you taken the laudanum?""Yes, I'm feeling much better, my Lord.""Do you think you are well enough to come downstairs, my dear? " At his words, her face glowed like a child at Christmas, and she gushed happily."Of course I am! I am bloody well tired of lying in this bed all morning! I-" On realizing her gaffe, however, she colored up instantly, her cheeks taking on a red tinge as she stared in horror at the bed covers, which she was clutching tightly with both hands.Trying to control his mirth, James dismissed the scandalized maids with a look, sitting next to his wife on the bed as the door shut quietly behind them.And laughed. Olivia was stunned by the rich sound and she realized that it was so rare for him to laugh, that it took the one who had the privilege of witnessing it by surprise. What had made him so pensive?As his laughter subsided, he put his arms around her shoulders and pulled her close, murmuring softly."My dear, you constantly surprise and delight me. Who would have thought that such a lady like voice could make the word bloody sound like a compliment?" Noticing her embarrassment however, he took hold of both her hands, rubbing circles on them with his thumbs, urging her silently to look up at him.She did so after a few seconds, and the soft smile on his face coaxed out one of her own, and after a long time, she felt relaxed with her husband."Now let us get your injured self into a proper gown. We have a-"Before James could complete his sentence however, the door burst open and a gentleman walked in proclaiming loudly, "Jamie boy, how long are you going to take to meet me downstairs? I am your guest after all, am I not?"On seeing them though, he appeared gobsmacked for a moment as he blinked a few times and cleared his throat awkwardly. James had stood up at that and with a quick "I shall see you downstairs in a few minutes, Olivia." ,and a harsh look for the intruder, whom he practically dragged from the room.After two minutes of inactivity, the two maids entered the room urging her to choose a gown to wear for meeting the 'guest' downstairs. Snapping out of her puzzlement, she rose from the bed to go to her dressing room, feeling like looking beautiful for Ja mes.***James pulled Connie into the study and slammed the door behind them, turning to face his friend."What was so important that you couldn't wait for me to come to you?" he thundered."How was I supposed to know you had a mistress installed at Bentham? As far as I knew, you didn't even have a mistress! James!" The last words were choked out as James had picked him up by his collar holding him up to the wall."She is my wife, the countess of Winchester, and you shall address her as such!"A well aimed kick at his leg made him drop his friend back onto the floor, who smoothened his collar while walking towards the brandy snifter on the table and taking a gulp before saying, "I apologize.""I apologize as well..... It is just that she is... special to me. With her, I feel like my past can be forgotten, and replaced with a better future. But Connie, she was shot on our wedding day."Connie whirled around at his words, his happiness at the first words replaced with rage and horror at the conclusion that his best friend's wife was being targeted by the very traitor that he and James were searching for. There could be no other explanation."What do we do?"James looked at his friend pensively, trying in vain to think of some way to protect Olivia from the traitor, apart from him staying away from her, which was

unpalatable to him, and he was starting to think, quite impossible."I want you to keep an eye on her, Connie. Her proximity to me only increases her danger. But maintaining a distance from her might give the wrong idea to everyone, which is something I do not want her to face. Also, she happens to possess some papers of relevance to our search, and I must subtly try to get them from her without arousing her suspicion. Which is a rather daunting task in itself. The woman could pass off as a spy any day!"Connie laughed at James face, "Looks like you've met your match, Jamie. She seems spirited enough, even for you!" This smart remark earned him a smack on the head, which he took graciously, apart from his raucous laughter at his friend's red cheeks.Suddenly the door to the study opened, and the very object of their discussion stepped in, every inch the haughty countess, and said in a cool tone, "So I was right in assuming the room where you two gentlemen were to be found would be the one where all the noise would be coming from. Shall we proceed to the dining room, my Lord? Your friend must be hungry from his travels."So saying, she turned and left the room as gracefully as she had entered, the pastel pink satin of her gown barely making a sound to disturb the awkward silence that encompassed the room."Is this the same woman you were talking about, James ?" Connie asked quizzically, eyeing his friend's posture, which had turned slightly rigid. But James was as puzzled as Connie and no answer came forth from his lips, but he left the room instantly, leaving a befuddled Conrad to follow him to the dining room.***
**When she reached the dining room, Olivia stopped at the threshold

for a second. Spy? Met your match? What had she heard? Was there any truth to all of it, and if so, what was she getting into? All these thoughts crashed inside her head.She had overheard the two men talking, and had foolishly barged in on them, when she could have heard much more without them knowing. But it had gone against her morals, and this fight going on in her heart had affected her mood and made her voice come out cool as ice. Oh dear, what must their guest think!It was obvious that he was a good friend of James, and she had offended them both. Not knowing how long they would take, she went and took a seat to the right of James seat, preparing what she would say to apologize.James entered the room a few seconds later, and stopped at the sight of his Siren sitting at the table, eyes closed, as if in deep thought. Walking to the table, he saw that she was slowly massaging her injured side, wincing as she touched a sore spot."Olivia?"Her eyes popped open at his voice and she stood up to face him, saying ,"I am so sorry, James. He is obviously a good friend of yours, and I just barged in on your conversation, forgetting all my manners! It was a dreadful mistake on my part, and I have shamed you. Please forgive me! " ,after which she became completely silent, staring at him with pleading eyes."It is alright my dear. You have done nothing to make me feel ashamed, so you needn't fret so. But I would like to speak to you in private later. Conrad will be staying for a few days atleast, I believe. And are you really feeling well enough? Does it hurt too much?""No my lord. I will be fine." She smiled at her Pirate, touched by his concern, and realized that she must have been rubbing the wound as she was wont to do, and he must have seen it.Conrad came into the room just then, and the couple turned to him with identical smiles, though James seemed a bit strained compared to Olivia's bright one. Vowing to continue their earlier conversation sometime later, Connie prepared to enjoy lunch with his best friend and his wife.

Chapter 23

Conrad stretched lazily,getting out of the bed in the guest room at Bentham and walking to the window. What greeted him was a view of an elegant black steed thundering into the adjoining forest, with who he assumed was James on his back.

If he was a normal newly wed man, he wouldn't be awake so early in the morning, let alone be riding away from his wife as if the hounds of hell were after him. Sighing, he turned away from the window, ringing for hot water for a bath.

Yesterday's lunch had been a raucous affair, him automatically switching on his charm to make the countess, or rather Olivia, as she had insisted he call her, feel at ease. It had worked upto an extent with her responding to his tales of James as a child with an enthusiasm he had not expected her to show this early in the marriage.

Since then, he had spent his time observing the couple and he had, in the course of his astute observations, recognized a certain tension, and at the same time a great deal of light heartedness in their interactions. There were a few tense moments, as when he had asked how they had come to be wed, at which there had been a pointed silence that descended on the room.

He had been thinking of the documents that she apparently had, and wondered what documents could a woman possibly possess of relevance to the identification of a traitor.

As the maids brought buckets of water to fill the tub placed in the adjoining suite, he paced the room, eager to get his friend rid of all the problems that had descended on his already complicated life. But what could he do?

A ride after his bath sounded like just the thing to clear his mind. Maybe then he'd be able to think of something.

****

Just a few doors down from Connie, Olivia sat at her escritoire, rereading the letter she had written to her parents. Did she sound too happy? Or too sad? Should she tell them about Conrad?

Dear God, now she was obsessing over a letter to her parents! What was wrong with her?

Folding the letter, she put in in an envelope, and sealed it, placing it to the side, mentally making a note to give it to the butler later.

She had heard James leave his suite about half an hour ago. He had been disturbed since the arrival of his friend, and she had seen them converse in low tones throughout the day when they thought she wasn't paying attention.

To add to the turbulence of her thoughts, last night she had dreamt of the papers on Lord Radnor that Willie had given her to peruse. In the dream, she had opened up the papers, and had found them stained red. The room where she was, was dark and a storm raged outside, the windows rattling ominously.

Normally she would have never believed in such a dream, but in light of recent events, her mind would not let go of it.

Getting up, she walked to the chest placed at the foot of her bed, and rummaging in it, took out the brown paper parcel. Briefly she contemplated throwing it in the fire, but realized her foolishness almost instantly. Opening the wrap, she quickly scanned through the papers once more, even though any salient points that she thought could be useful had been noted down by her.

She couldn't help but feel that this wrapped bundle was of some importance to her, and must be kept safely. Though now she had no means to explore the mysterious travels of the Duke, she thought helplessly.

Perhaps she could speak to James about her doubts? He seemed like someone who would listen to what she had to say without reprimanding her too much for her actions. But she still had the fear of trusting anybody with the information she had acquired. But he was her husband, was he not? She would speak to him later in the afternoon, probably after lunch.

Satisfied with her decision, and feeling a little weight lifted of her shoulders after a long time, she picked up her letter, making her way downstairs to find the butler.

****

James urged Sultan to go a little faster through the undergrowth, his own eyes already stinging because of the dust and dirt flying into them. He knew he was taking the horse a bit too far, but the ride always helped him clear his head of any clutter, and many a time, even helped him find the answers to many of the problems he had to face.

They had helped him this time as well, and he was now on his way back to Bentham, after an hour long ride through the forests surrounding the estate. His first priority now was to speak to Olivia about the papers she had in her possession. He would also wish to ask her about why she had them in the first place, but that was secondary to actually acquiring the information. That would aid him in the search for that bastard who had thought of harming his Siren.

Even in the liberation he was feeling at the ride, he was barely conscious of a few nicks and cuts he had sustained from briars that he hadn't avoided in time. But it was all worth it in the end.

As the stocky structure of Bentham started to come into view, he reduced Sultan's speed to a canter, murmuring to the horse as he always did after a hard ride. Trotting to the stables, he dismounted, handing the reins to a groom and instructing him to give the steed a good rub down and a trough of fresh water after some time.

Just then his head groom, Manson walked over to him and told him that the countess would like him to wait here for a few moments for her as she wished to speak to his Lordship. Thanking the groom for the information, he went to the side entrance of the house to wait for his wife.

And hoped she'd get something to eat, if only an apple. He was ravenous.

****

As it was, Olivia was at that moment, waiting in the kitchens for Mrs. Trout to hand her the picnic basket she had asked for, as she had thought James would be hungry after his ride. Also, it would give them some time alone to talk about the papers away from the house as well, which was something she preferred, compared to the formal environment within the walls of Bentham.

The bustling cook came back happily brandishing a basket that contained something that smelled positively heavenly. She wanted to take a peek at the contents, but managed to control herself, giggling at her own behaviour softly.

Thanking the rotund woman, she set off towards the side entrance into the rose garden, her blue gown swishing softly around her. It was a bit different from her usual style, the bodice was a criss-crossed pattern of dark blue fabric, cinched at the waist, the lower half flowing magnificently to the ground. The sleeves were the main attraction of the gown, made of light blue transparent crepe that was unstitched on the inner aspect, which made it whisper along her skin as she walked.

Her hair had been braided on her scalp, but was loose over her shoulders, held together by tiny sapphire pins. Her colour was slightly flushed due to the heat of the kitchens and her own rush to reach her husband.

So it was this flushed and radiantly beautiful Siren that greeted James as he lounged on a cherub fountain in the rose garden. Basket in one hand and a brown parcel in the other, she came through the glass panelled doors of the house, and James found himself once again caught in her spell.

Walking towards her, he saw her look up at him and her step faltered a bit, before she righted it and smiled at him, causing him to walk closer, freeing her hand of the basket to lift it to his lips.

"You look radiant this morning, my love. I see you've decided to make a picnic out of breakfast?", he queried laughingly.

"Would you prefer to have it inside, my Lord? If so, we shall go inside, I do not mind."

"No, my dear, it is perfectly alright. I have heard you wish to speak to me about something, so we shall speak as we breakfast. Come along."

They walked towards a nearby oak tree, spreading the blanket from the basket on the ground and taking a seat on it.

As they ate the fresh bread and cheese, apples and oranges and even a slice of pound cake, Olivia showed him the parcel, explaining the reason why she obtained it, the information she had gained from it and her fears of it, even the dream she had had.

James listened to all she had to say in silence, wondering if he should tell her he wanted the information himself, and the reasons he wanted it for, that he was a spy, that the duke was probably the person due to which she was attacked on their wedding day and that the man was probably a traitor to England. But however much he thought, the only answer that came to him was that she shouldn't know. At least until the traitor was caught. It would keep her safe.

"Olivia, I accept what you have done wholeheartedly, and I won't reprimand you for your actions. However, I would wish you tell me about anything else of this nature that occurs, or any other suspicions you may have. I would wish to keep this with me. I might be able to deduce some more information, or bring some more clarity to this riddle with the help of a few resources I possess. I will of course, keep you updated of any progress in the matter." So she would only know what he wished her to know, and it would increase her protection, he thought to himself.

Olivia thought he was offering her a fair deal. She knew that she couldn't possibly have the 'resources' a man of the ton had, and his way would be faster to obtain the answers which she wanted.

"Thank you, James. You have lifted a weight of my shoulders and I am grateful for it. I would very well expect updates from you, though.", she ended, smiling.

"You have my word, my dear. Shall we leave for home? I shall send a servant to get the basket."

Agreeing on that, the couple walked away from their picnic, completely unaware of a pair of eyes that watched them furtively a few trees away.

The watcher straightened from his crouch and smiled sinisterly. It would be fun to play a prank on the Winchesters.

Indeed it would.

Chapter 24

Olivia watched as James entered the parlor where she and Conrad were waiting for him. It was tea time and she had asked both men to be present as she was bored with her own company and wished to enjoy a good cup of tea with two people she could trust....one of whom was her husband.

After their picnic, she had wandered off to the library in search of a good book and had spent her time reading till lunch time. After tea, perhaps she would go back to her book of poetry. It seemed very promising, though the author was anonymous. It was something that intrigued her, but then again, what could she do to trace the poet?

Banishing her thoughts for sometime, she smiled at her husband as he gave her a customary kiss on her hand, before going to sit on the couch opposite her, with Connie.

"What took you so long, Jamie boy? Must you make me wait for my daily dose of tea, then?" Conrad said, with a smirk on his face.

"I just had a few papers to attend to, is all. 'Dose' of tea, eh? I can assure you, my wife brews an excellent cup of tea, one that will most certainly leave you begging for more.", James replied, stunning his friend into silence and making his wife blush at the compliment.

She stuttered slightly, "That is enough, my Lord. Ignore all of that please, Conrad. How would you like your tea?"

James watched as she poured for Connie, handing him the cup and saucer, before automatically pouring his tea the way he liked it. As she held up his cup in front of him, he slowly slid his hand along hers before grasping the saucer and looking into her eyes. The awareness that passed between them was brief but palpable. It would have lasted longer, but for an exclamation from Connie.

"Ah, such flavour! Such a rich taste! Madam, I believe you have taught me to love our national beverage!" Picking up Olivia's hand, he brought it to his lips across the tea-table, causing her to lurch slightly forward and James to bristle angrily.

"I believe it would be better for your well-being, puppy, if you let go of my wife's hand this instant." James ground out through his teeth.

Taking a look at James face, Connie let go of Olivia's hand, staring thoughtfully at his friend's face for a moment, before smiling to himself and picking up his cup. Olivia thanked him softly and poured herself a cup of tea, sipping it quietly.

Conrad left them after a few minutes, and Olivia stood up, intending to excuse herself to go complete the book of anonymous poetry, but James's voice stopped her.

"It's 'Conrad' now, is it?" he said, sneering the word slightly.

"I do not know what you mean, James", she said, though she was starting to think she did know.

"Oh please ignore me, I'm just your husband. Why give me any importance at all?"

"Would you please stop acting like a child? I don't even understand what I've done wrong when you get angry with me! I never try to do anything to anger you, but you always seem to be on the brink of losing patience with me!" she shouted.

"Olivia, just leave. We shall talk later. For now, just leave."

Humiliated beyond belief, Olivia turned around with a sob, walking out of the room as fast as her feet would take her. Going to the library, she picked up her book from where she had left it before. Then she rushed to the staircase, climbing it furiously, almost tripping in her rush to reach her room. How could he be so unbelievably rude? Had he no concern for her feelings? Getting jealous like this was not good for anybody, especially since there was no reason to feel so! She never could dream of being unfaithful to her Pirate! But why couldn't he understand that?

With these thoughts tumbling in her head, she entered her chamber quickly. But before she could close the doors, someone or something hit her on the head with a great force. Clutching her head, she watched helplessly as the ground rushed up to meet her face.

****

The Countess really was heavy. But that could probably be attributed to her gown's fabric. In any case, he had almost reached his destination. Pushing open the door in front of him, he laid the bound and gagged body in his arms on the floor roughly.

It had been a bit of clever thinking on his part, bringing her here. It would teach that arrogant Earl a lesson he'd never forget. Plus it added to the excitement of the hunt for him, he thought, and if anyone could have seen the evil look on his face, they would probably shudder in fear at the hint of madness that glinted in his eyes.

Oh, but he must leave soon. No use dawdling here, his work was done. It had been too easy to knock out the chit. After all, no one expected a criminal to come inside their house, let alone enter their bedchamber!

Resisting the urge to laugh at the foolishness of people's thoughts, he extracted the piece of paper from his coat pocket, removing one of the pins from her hair, to fasten it on her gown. Turning up the collar of his greatcoat, he left the way he had come, whistling slightly.

It was a beautiful day after all.

****

James looked up from the papers that Olivia had given him to the clock that declared it had been two hours since she had left the parlour. He really should go and apologize. She might have calmed down like he had, and would not make him grovel too much, though God knew he should, since he could not help but behave like a complete idiot when she so much as looked at another man with a smile. It was ridiculous, he knew, but he'd be damned if he knew how to control it.

Chapter 25

James stumbled to a halt at the base of the staircase, bellowing at the top of his voice. "Pemberly!"

The middle aged butler rushed in from the foyer, alarmed at the urgency in his master's voice. "Yes, my lord?", he asked, though James was clearly about to tell him exactly what the matter was.

"Where is her Ladyship?", James ground out, clearly controlling his anger.

"I do not know specifically, my lord. But she hasn't left the house, my lord.", Pemberly said. "I shall ask the footmen to look for her ladyship at once." So saying, he barked at the waiting footmen, who had come after hearing the commotion."Search all the rooms for the countess, and inform us of her whereabouts. Four of you will search upstairs, the remaining four of you and myself shall take care of the rooms on this floor, even the kitchen and the servant's quarters. Move fast!"

At his words, the footmen sprang into action, each one eager to find their mistress. Pemberly turned to James. "My lord -"

Surprisingly, he was cut off by Connie, who had been standing just behind James after he was alerted to come out from his room.

"Pemberly, James and myself will check outdoors if we can find her ladyship. Kindly notify us of any developments that may occur." At this, he started pulling James towards the doors leading to the gardens.

Just after a few steps however, a foot man hailed them from above. "My lords, I believe you should come and see this. In her ladyship's room."

James needed no further prompting. He sprinted for the stairs, Connie in close pursuit.

What could I have missed seeing in her room? Could it be a farewell letter? Had she abandoned him?

With these torturous thoughts crashing in his mind James took the stairs two at a time, racing into her room to find the footman, Russell, he believed the lad was named, pointing at a book lying on the floor. Walking towards it, James realized what he was looking at. How did she find this?

But now there were other, more important matters at hand. Picking up the slim volume, he turned to Connie, who was looking worried. At James almost imperceptible nod, however, he turned quickly and rushed out of the room.

James thanked the footman, giving him orders to have Bentham house searched in every nook and cranny till the countess was located.

Then he left the way Connie had. Out the front door.

****

For the third time in just so many days, Olivia woke up in unfamiliar surroundings. This had to stop, she thought.

But as her attention was taken away from her surroundings, she was shocked to feel the gag in her mouth, one that smelled like it had been retrieved from the nether regions of a horse. Forcing herself to stop thinking about that happy bit of information and take the damn thing off, she was dismayed to know that she couldn't feel her hands! And come to think of it, she couldn't feel her legs too!

Peering at where her hands were supposed to be, she saw they had been bound tightly together, enough to bruise her skin. Her legs were the same.

And her head felt like the devil itself had taken up residence, and was banging on every spot he could see.

She calmly recalled how she had been hit on the head before. What time was it? Where was she? Why was she tied up? Would her captor be coming back? What did he want with her?

After all these thoughts, there came just one.

James.

Oh, what she would give to see his dear face! He would search for her, she was sure. But did he know she was gone yet? Had he been harmed too? That sent chills down her spine, and gave her courage.

She must escape this place and get to her Pirate.

She started to work on the bindings on her hands.

****

James guided Sultan to Bentham Park, passing the horse to a waiting groom. He was at his wits end. It had been more than an hour since he and Connie hadsearched the entire land under Bentham, even the village. Where could he take her? James had even searched the book to see if it had any clue or even a missive from the kidnapper. There was nothing.

Staring at the retreating back of Sultan, James silently thanked the beast for his stamina, as he had made him gallop through the surrounding brush without care. The steed had been lazing in the corral with Connie's horse before they had come to know about Olivia's abduction, but when James had coaxed him to give his all, the stallion had not shied or tried to throw him. He was greatful for that.

Suddenly he was struck by a thought.

"Hell and damnation!" the curse was out of his lips and he raced towards the stables, knowing his last hope rested there.

****

She almost had the rope off her hands.

The only reason that she was taking so much time, was that the feeling had returned to her abused hands as soon as she had begun to free her hands. And the pain was beyond anything she had imagined. She was thankful for the gag, foul odour or not. It kept her from screaming out loud.

The only reason she was silently trying to free herself was James. She couldn't let their last words to each other be in anger. She couldn't live without him.

She loved him.

****

Olivia heard foot steps thundering closer to her spot on the hay, and it was all she could do to keep from screaming in agony at her plight. Whoever came along with those footfalls, she thought, is going to get the worst treatment she was capable of. Steeling her veins and murmuring a small apology to James, she looked to the door.

And her tears flowed freely down her cheeks at the sight she saw.

****

James fell to his knees at the sight of his Siren lying on the hay, hands and legs bound, mouth gagged with a piece of filthy cloth. Their eyes met, and she closed hers as the tears spilled onto her cheeks. He might have shed a few himself.

James had never thanked the Lord with as much fervor as he did when he held Olivia in his arms that day.

Chapter 26

James fingered the note he had found on Olivia's gown the day he had rescued her from the stables. It had been three days since, and according to the note, just a day before he had to meet the perpetrator of the attacks on his wife's life. The missive was simply worded –

Winchester,

This time I let her live. The next time, who can say?

Meet me five days from now, at the place and time where your dearest mother took her last breath.

It is only fitting that you do the same.

-C

Unfortunately, Olivia had been the one to notice it first after he had untied her and helped her stand up. Now he could not hide the facts about his mother from her. Though she had been very discreet by not asking him anything, he knew that he owed it to her to tell her the entire story, even about him being a spy, since that was what had got her into so much trouble in the first place.

He was at that moment, waiting for her to come to his study. They had arrived at his town house the previous evening, and the news of their arrival had spread like wildfire, and the silver salver Pemberly had brought to them at breakfast had been piled high with invitations to every ball and soiree taking place in the next seven days.

Olivia had looked at them fleetingly, smiled at the number of them, and resumed eating her toast. Puzzled at her behavior, James had queried her and she had replied simply, " We can attend as many events as we like, but after we catch him."

He had tried to dissuade her from getting involved in this as it was extremely dangerous, but she had firmly ignored him and continued doing whatever she had been doing before he had spoken. He hadn't the heart, nor the will to argue with her, so he had brought her along with him.

Just then a knock sounded on the door."Enter", said James, rising to his feet when as Olivia swept into the room, dressed today in a day dress of lavender silk, a clever little hat placed on her head. She had purchased it on Bond street just a few days before their marriage, and had longed to wear it since. James looked properly appreciative of her attire, his gaze making a slow sweep from her head to her toe, making her squirm slightly.

"Madam wife, allow me to tell you how beautiful you look today. I can scarcely breathe, you look so gorgeous." Walking towards her, James was assailed by the flowery scent that always seemed to accompany her wherever she went. The scent he had come to identify as Olivia's own.

She was trying valiantly to hold back her blush, staring determinedly at the floor. He so rarely got to see her so flustered, and he loved that he was the one to make her feel so.

James put a finger to her chin, gently forcing her to look up.

And was undone at the emotion in her eyes.

****

Olivia wondered how it was that a simple compliment from her pirate had the ability to make her heart flop around in her chest like a fish out of water. Oh, how she loved this man. But how could she tell him? After all, everyone knew that men of the ton never married for love. This line of thought, brought a sheen of tears to her eyes, but she stopped herself before she shed any of them.

Just then her husband tipped her chin up, and the desire she saw in his warm gaze fanned the fires of her own. She had never known herself to be such a wanton, never had any other gentleman made her feel this way. Maybe it was just James. Just her pirate.

When he lowered his lips to hers, she breathed in the warm musky scent that was as much a part of him as his piercing grey eyes and raven black locks. He ran a hand from the nape of her neck to her lower back, making her shiver. Applying a little pressure, the remaining distance between them vanished and her hands came up to tangle in his hair reveling in its soft texture.

This time he didn't have to ask for entrance into the sweet cave of honey that was her mouth. As the pleasure built, Olivia deepened the kiss by herself pulling him impossibly closer, as if to blend them into one being. James deep growl of pleasure, however elicited a giggle from her mouth.

James was not happy the kiss had ended. Jerking Olivia to him, he asked, "What amuses you so darling?"

His voice came out gruff, but Olivia was not deterred. Staring endearingly at him she replied, "I love you, James."

James felt as if there was no air left in the room. She loved him? Him? Love? But before he could think any further, She laid a hand on his cheek, saying softly, "James, do not be alarmed. Love is not a burden, it is something that sets you free. Even if you do not love me, it does not matter. Even if you care for me a little, I shall be content."

He replied harshly, "Of course I care for you Olivia!" Overwhelmed by the palpable emotions in the room, he crushed her tightly to his chest, as if he never wanted to let her go. For now, this is enough, thought Olivia, smiling against his jacket.

After a few moments of standing close together, Olivia piped up ."What about that dastardly man James? What are we going to do about him? "

James sighed. She was not going to let it go this easily. He would have to leave her behind tomorrow, though he knew she would insist on coming. And he could not bear to put her in harm's way one more time. His nerves would not be able to withstand it one more time. But for now he had to tell her about his mother.

"Olivia, come with me."With one last kiss on her forehead, he led her to the divan placed near the window and drew her to sit beside him, thinking of how to tell her that he had killed his mother.

Olivia was quietly sitting on the diwan next to her husband, wondering at his sombre expression. It did not bode well for the conversation, she knew, because she had rarely seen him thus.

James eyes had taken on a faraway look, as if he had been transported to a time beyond her comprehension. His mouth was set in a straight line as he stared unblinking through the window, and it was beginning to startle her. "James?", she called out softly touching his hand with her own.

James turned to face her then, eyes now cleared of their previous emotion. Abruptly he stood, letting out a shaky breath and pacing a few steps away from her. She longed to urge him to come back, but knew instinctively that he needed the distance to collect himself for whatever he planned to say to her, so she remained silent.

"My mother was a tiny woman, constantly cowed by my over bearing father. Theirs was a classic union of two families for wealth and social standing. My mother, Eunice, was not very happy, but she had to do it for the sake of her family's honour. So she did. My father did his duty and planted a seed in her, and I was born a year after their marriage." James paused, to let those words sink, and continued.

"Everything was going on as it does in every titled lord's house till the year I turned nine. My mother had a passion for poetry, and she used to dabble in the art herself, even reading a few of her milder works to me once or twice. My father had no knowledge of this, as he would never have approved of flowery notions like poetry. He used to diligently handle the Winchester estates, and had no time for a wife and child who was his heir.

Oh he took care of us, do not mistake me. But never was there a kind word spoken or praise given when deserved. He hardly ever turned up for meals, even. My mother, started growing bolder at his ignorance, however. She was not accustomed to contacting the ladies of the ton, as they were barely civil since she was wealthy but not titled before marriage. She only had me to talk to, a child of nine.

She told me of her poetry, how it set her free, buoyed her spirits. How much she enjoyed it. I too was happy listening to her talk of her love for the subject. It became a daily pastime of ours, to sit and talk about poetry whenever I was free from my lessons for the day.

But one day she came home from a carriage ride, looking dazed and slightly winded. She saw me standing at the foot of the stairs, and pulled me into a nearby room, telling me to sit and listen. I still remember what she said to me that day.

"James", she said, "I met someone today! A most exciting, compelling man! We sat together and spoke for hours. He too loves poetry like me, perhaps even more so! We discussed so much together, our likes, dislikes, all of our life even! Oh James dear, it was perfect!"

I of course, thought it was acceptable for my mother to speak to other people, never mind that it was a man. So I listened like I always did, my love for my wayward mother, shining in my eyes. After all she was the one that was always with me, even though my father was not.

For a month, her stories about her 'mystery man' continued, and I continued to think nothing of it, though even I had begun to have my own suspicions as her descriptions were becoming different, and she cut off her sentences more often, refusing to tell me any thing even if I prodded her to.

One day she just let slip that she was going to meet him in the evening the next day, and that I should not worry if she did not come home till the next day. I was worried, but how could I tell her? The stars in her eyes were too hard to depress. My father was not in London for a few days as he had business in the country, which was probably adding to my mother's boldness.

The day after, she left in the evening, looking beautiful and radiant, after giving me a kiss on my forehead and instructing me to be a good boy. I waved at her carriage through the window, but who knows if she even saw me in her excitement to reach her beloved. I was in my room upstairs, being prepared for bed, when I was summoned downstairs by loud voices. Or rather, just one voice."

Olivia closed her eyes and breathed out,"Your father."

"Indeed it was.His business had concluded earlier than he had anticipated, and he was home, in the flesh. Though I still wonder if some one had tipped him off about my mother's activities, or if he had been monitoring them all along, biding his time till she made a fatal miscalculation. But that is a story for another day. My father was home, and he was demanding to know the whereabouts of his wife. None of the servants could tell where she had gone, no one knew. No one except me.

Now, when me and my mother had spoken every day, we had totally underestimated my father, assuming he knew nothing of our talks. But he always knew. Always knew that his wife never spoke to any of the ladies, but only to me. That I probably knew all of her secrets, because my mother was so desperately in need of someone to tell her adventures to, or else she would have certainly caved in under the pressure of holding it all in.

Long story short, my father called me to his study and eventually got the truth out of me. In the end I was so damn weak that one of the footmen had to carry me up to my chamber. But my father was still waiting.

My mother came in the next morning at seven, and was informed of my father's return. I had not been able to sleep a wink, and had left my room at five in the morning to wait for my mother to come home. Standing at the top of the stairs, I saw my mother's face turn ashen at the news, but as my father came out of the study, it was as if she was reborn.

Any of her previous fear was replaced by something brave. As if she knew some thing we all did not and was exalted at the thought. Calmly she sailed by my father into his study. And my father followed.

I had been holding my breath for the entire time but as the click of the lock on the door echoed throughout the silent house, I knew something terrible was to happen. So I ran to that door. And pushed it open slightly.

My parents were standing apart, facing each other, and my mother was smiling. There was something about that smile, that caused goosebumps to erupt on my skin. She said, " So you know now what I have been doing all these days while you tended to your precious lands."

My father was livid with fury." You bitch! How dare you speak to me thus? "

"Don't you see? I do not fear you anymore, you can do nothing that will make me regret doing what I have done with my life. All your threats and vile words are for naught.", she replied, still smiling complacently.

"I will kill you, whore!" My father walked menacingly towards her but she shook her head. "No, it is I who will take my own life. It shall not be tainted by a beast like you."

So saying, she reached into her reticule, pulling out a small object which she swallowed, much to my horror. I couldn't bear it any longer. I thrust open the door and ran to my mother.

"Shhh, dear boy. Don't cry. You must always be happy, promise me that no matter what your sire says, you will always endeavour to find happiness even though you will have to go against him. Promise me, child.", she whispered , leaning down to my level and stroking my hair.

Not knowing what to do, I nodded mutely, tears flowing down my cheeks, as I realized that my mother was going to die now, because of me.

My father came up to us and pushed me out of the way. I fell to the ground roughly , banging my head on the floor. The last thing I remembered was my father's voice screaming profanities at my mother.

I woke up in the evening in my room, and the maid informed me that my mother had been laid to rest without a funeral in someplace no one knew.

Somehow, I couldn't even bring myself to cry at my loss. I was just too numb to feel any pain.

My father and I never spoke after the incident, except of course, when my father wished to insult me or reprimand me. He hated me ever since. Actually, I hated myself, for failing to protect the one person who was always there for me." James paused, afraid to even look at Olivia to see the revulsion and hatred on her beautiful face, condemning him like no other person could.

Olivia however, let out a small cry of anguish, and leapt off the diwan, running towards him and enclosing him in her arms.

Chapter 27

James felt the impact as Olivia collided against his back, wrapping her arms around his waist. Slowly separating her from him, he turned to face her, tipping up her chin slightly. The anger blazing in the green depths caught him off guard.

"How dare he? How dare they both?! If they weren't already dead, I would- ", she breathed, cutting herself short to declare," No child deserves to go through that, James. No child."Moving away from him toward the windows, she spoke again.

"You are the bravest and most courageous man I have known. I – I feel ashamed of my privileged childhood. I do not know if I could survive what you did, without shattering emotionally. I promise you, my Pirate, you shall never have to suffer through anything like that ever again. After tomorrow, I will never let anything come in the way of our happiness. Ever."

Before James could say anything further, a voice spoke loudly.

"Not if I can help it, darling."

****

She sat in a secret corridor of the house, wondering how to do what she had come to do. She had seen him pass by her hiding spot a few times since she had arrived, and her throat had closed up at the sight of him and tears had filled her eyes.

It hadn't been long since her husband had died, and his loss had saddened her like no other. But they had spoken of death for a long time and she was prepared mentally for what was to follow.

Her darling Daniel had departed the world a scarce week ago, and she had been planning her visit since then. But she wasn't as courageous as she believed herself to be, as she kept coming through the passage, but never could speak to the one person she was dying to meet. And she couldn't have peace without the meeting.

It would be a closure of sorts, speaking to him. But she had to gird her loins and approach him for that. Was she ready for this?

Walking back through the passage she came to an intersection, one leading to the back of the house, where she had entered from. Suddenly she came to a decision, and taking a deep breath, started down the other pathway. Maybe it would not be as bad as she feared it would be. Just maybe.....

****

"Radnor." James spoke as if it was a usual occurrence for a member of the ton to step out of the shadows in his study. With a gun pointed at his heart.

The study was a large room, with one wall full of shelves for the various books on management and law that the Earls had accumulated over the years. There was a liquor cabinet standing in between the bookshelf and James desk and chair which were set in the middle of the spacious room, with a set of armchairs adjacent to it. Radnor had been hiding behind the liquor cabinet, biding his time. How he had managed to get there, was a mystery.

Inside he was quivering with anger and fear for Olivia's safety. He could not be sure that the bastard wouldn't kill Olivia after him. Or do something much worse than that.

No, he couldn't think about that now. He had to focus on keeping Olivia and himself alive. But how was Albansdale involved? He tried to think... had he encountered him anywhere in the Office? But he could come up with nothing to connect the man to everything that had occurred.

"That's le tueur to you Winchester.", Matthew smirked, looking at James as his head snapped up attentively.

"I wondered why you had been travelling to France so much in the past few years, and now I have my answer. 'The killer', is it?", Olivia spoke, smirking a little as his smile dropped instantly.

"Olivia-", James said, starting towards her, a warning on his face. She was puzzled by that, but decided to comply. After all he seemed more experienced in the field. Everything was becoming a bit more clearer in her mind. But she was furious to realize that Duke Radnor had been the one to harm her both those times. Slowly she placed her hand at the side of her skirts, feeling the hard object kept there to reassure herself that she was prepared to attack if needed.

"Someone has been a busy little bee, eh? Step away from her Winchester. We wouldn't want a stray bullet to hit her, would we now?"

"You despicable beast."Olivia's voice was barely a whisper, but it caught the Duke's attention.

"Watch your tongue, bitch! One more word and I will do as I please. You think you are so clever don't you? But I am even more so."By the tenor of his voice, and the slight sheen of sweat that had developed on his forehead, James could see that the man was not in a stable state of mind. Probably had taken some alcohol to fortify himself before he came. He tried to think of a way to finish this before it became nasty. He wished that Connie had been nearby. Just then the Duke spoke again," By the by Winchester, how is the scar?", he said, turning to James once more.

"Of no importance. But tell me why you did it? The W.O. has been onto you for a while, and so it seems, has my wife. We would have caught you in a few days. Why turn a traitor to your country, Radnor?"

"That, my friend, is inconsequential. But why don't you tell your wife about your career? I'm sure we would both love to hear about that."

James looked at Olivia, trying to gauge her reaction. She was looking at him steadily, no trace of an accusation in her eyes, as if she would never judge him based on someone else's information. He was grateful.

"Olivia, I-" he began.

"Bloody hell, I don't have time for this!", the intruder bellowed, aiming his pistol at James with a glint of madness in his eyes.

"No James!", cried Olivia, beginning to rush to his side, her eyes wide with fear. But before anything else could happen, the Duke gave a cry of pain, his eyes rolling back in his head as his large form crumpled to the ground in a heap.

And James world shook to the core as he saw the figure standing behind the now unconscious duke.

"Mother?"

Chapter 28

"James," said the tiny woman, lowering the table-lamp she was clutching in her hands shakily. Her eyes had a sheen of tears, and her fragile lips seemed to tremble with the effort of keeping her tears in. Her clothes were simple, a grey day dress with black trim and no flounces and a bonnet sat slightly askew on her head, so different from what James remembered her wearing when she- was alive? Was his mother? It seemed laughable now. What was he supposed to think? To feel? How had she survived? His father had known all along? Or hadn't he? James head spun sickeningly as he thought of all his life centered around this very moment.

Olivia watched every move of the woman suspiciously. This was James mother? The one who recited poetry to him and selfishly told him of her paramour? How could his mother be alive? After the entire story that James had told her..... She looked at her husband, noticing the ashen pallor of his skin and his shallow breathing. Oh dear.

"James! James!" Olivia said loudly while walking to him, hoping to get him out of the stupor he seemed to be in by startling him. Like a switch had been turned on inside him, his eyes cleared and focused on her, and she smiled slightly.

“I-Uh, we need to tie him up. And , um send word to the W.O. and Connie. Could you-“ James stuttered.

“I’ll go send the footmen, and ask for some strong rope,” Olivia said smoothly, giving a disgusted look to the sprawled form of the Duke, before turning to James again and touching his cheek, saying softly, ”Have courage, my lord. Everything has an explanation. I will be back soon.”

James wanted to tell her to stop, to stay with him, to help him face something he never thought he would have to face. But that would be cowardly. And what had she said? Have courage. So he would be courageous.

And speak to his mother.

****

Olivia first called the butler and asked for three footmen. Two she sent to fetch rope from the cellar, and she wrote a quick message to Connie, asking him to come over as they had caught the traitor and also to send word to the W.O., as she had no idea how to contact them, something both she and James had understandably overlooked before. Shaking her head, she asked the butler to tell the gentleman, or rather the gentlemen who came to wait in the Rose parlor.

When the two footmen came back with the rope, however, she decided the traitor would stay down for some more time. James shouldn’t be disturbed unless there arose unavoidable circumstances.

Ringing for a maid, she asked for a tea setting for three to be sent to the study posthaste. She needed to be beside her husband soon.

Work done, she sat down near the study door to wait for the tea tray.

****

"Mother, please have a seat, " he said, gesturing towards the diwan. He watched as she slowly stepped towards it, almost as if she was afraid he would do something to her. No, James thought, I am not my father. But you still deserve to suffer a bit for leaving me alone to deal with him. So he said nothing to her till she sat down, clutching her bonnet which she had taken off, in a death grip.

"James, I know what you must be thinking, or feeling-"

"No you don't! How-"

"Let me finish. I know, because I have had the same uncertainties since the past few days. I was-"

"Tell me how you are still alive."James said, his patience running thin. Did she think he would welcome her with open arms when she suddenly appeared like this? Without an explanation, she wouldn't even get his sympathy.

"Alright then, I will. That morning, the 'poison' I supposedly took, was actually a drug of some sort, that helps you fake your own death by suppressing your breath and heartbeats for a few minutes. After you fell unconscious, it took just a few seconds for the drug to produce its effects.

I knew your father would never suspect anything, he was too bent on seeing me die for my sins to even take notice of anything. As soon as he sent you to your room with a footman, he probably decided to get himself drunk, which was a blessing for me, because when I regained consciousness a few minutes later, he was half asleep at his desk, a half-empty bottle of Scotch next to him.

Without wasting any time, I scrambled to my feet, and escaped through the secret passage near the book shelf. Your father didn't even notice a thing." Taking a deep breath after the long narrative, his mother looked straight into his eyes, waiting for his next question.

James did not waste any time. "Where did you go? Where were you for all these years?" They both also knew his unsaid query. Why did you leave me?

"James, do you remember the man I told you about?" Eunice asked carefully.

"Your paramour, you mean? Yes, I remember all too clearly. Please continue." James said rudely, hating the way his voice sounded but he couldn't help it. He was just too angry to be reasonable.

Ignoring the pain his words caused, Eunice continued," His name was Daniel Marchbanks. He was an investor of sorts, and he also wrote beautiful poetry. He was, well, he was unmarried, and after meeting each other a few times we fell in love. I know I sound selfish, but I knew I wanted to be with him, just as I knew the best place for you was with your father. What could I have given you, James? With your father, you would be raised as his heir! That itself entitles an education, wealth, a reputation beyond reproach! What could I, a woman who resurrected herself to flee her husband the Earl, give you?"

"Love, mother. You could have given me love," whispered James.

Before his mother could reply, however, Olivia spoke.

"That is enough for now, my lord. The gentlemen await you in the Rose parlor." As both mother and son turned to her with equally shocked expressions, they hadn't heard her come in halfway through their conversation, she smiled soothingly.

"James dear, come along now. I shall send the footmen to take the duke to the parlor now. You must go greet our guests. I have sent a few snacks there, but you must leave. I shall keep her Ladyship company till you return." Olivia was trying to urge him along quickly, but at her last sentence, James stood abruptly.

"You shall not stay in the same room with her! I forbid it! As it is, she was on her way out," James ground out. And he meant every word. He wanted nothing more to do with the woman who had left him alone as a child.

"James, please, I will be safe. I promise," Olivia pleaded. She had to speak with the dowager. James was to unsettled to think clearly now, but she had to get him to understand. Suddenly she realized what she could do to allay his fears.

From the voluminous folds of her skirts, she unstrapped the small pistol she had started carrying with her and showed it to her husband, whose eyebrows rose high on his forehead. She laughed at his expression.

"Can you use that toy then?" James asked her, making her bristle.

"I will let you know that I am a crack shot, my lord," was the tart reply.

James smirked for a second before giving his mother a hard look that clearly warned her not to try anything while he was gone, she gave a curt nod in compliance.

"I will finish this business as soon as possible, my love, and come back to you. Also I shall send your lady's maid here, as a precaution," so saying, James kissed her forehead firmly, before striding to the door, his mind already thinking about what he was going to tell Nate, and how they were going to extract information from Radnor.

When the door shut behind the footmen who took the body with them, Olivia turned to the dowager and sat on the armchair opposite the diwan.

Looking at the woman before her, she smiled, "My lady, I shall introduce myself since my husband hasn't bothered to do so. I am Olivia Richardson, Countess Winchester and your son's wife."

Chapter 29

The atmosphere in the room was tense when James entered, mentally shedding the worry for Olivia, to give his full attention to the matter at hand.

Nate sat in one of the armchairs before the settee, two agents whom he recognized as Presley and Scott, two younger agents, flanking him. Conrad stood at the windows, gazing pensively through them. The tray of tea and snacks lay on the settee, untouched.

As soon as Nate entered, followed by the two footmen carrying the Duke, who placed him on one of the Rose upholstered wingback chairs, in a very uncomfortable position, Conrad turned away from his perusal of the street below.

"James! So it was Radnor, the son of a bitch!" he exclaimed, looking disdainfully at the sprawled form in the chair.

Nate nodded at James, his calm posture belying the churning that was going on in his gut. They had finally apprehended the traitor they had set out to find so long ago. Or rather, he had found them. He wanted to ask James if his lady was safe, but seeing as James was even in the room with them reassured him that she was.

As it was, James was about to tell them about all that had transpired that morning, leaving out the part about his mother knocking out the duke. That he could tell Connie and George later.

"Nate, should we discuss this now or later? It would ease my mind to know that the bastard was under lock and key, away from - everyone." James really didn't want to spend any more time than necessary on the traitor. Tomorrow was soon enough to tell Nate about everything.

"I agree, James. The bastard has already caused more than enough trouble for us all. I suggest you come by the office in the morning to file your official report. Conrad, you too." Nate gave them both a small smile, gesturing to the two young men that stood behind him, who promptly went to the unconscious man, checking the tightness of his bonds.

"Presley and Scott, take him round back to the carriage quietly. I shall join you shortly."

Nate stood up and walked to the door, stopping to shake hands with both Conrad and James.

"Very well done, both of you. Your hard work and diligence are commendable. But James, will I be losing an agent soon, then?" he queried sadly, looking him in the eyes.

"I believe not sir. Rather, there is another willing recruit for you."

All three men turned simultaneously towards the voice which had come from the door, where Olivia stood, smiling, with her hands folded demurely in front of her.

"I would like to be an agent for the crown, Mr. Nathaniel. And I would be honored ", she paused to take a breath at this juncture to look at her husband," if James would permit me to do so." She inwardly crossed her fingers, hoping James would agree. She knew she wanted to work as a spy, and really didn't want him to give up something he clearly enjoyed so much. Asking this so publicly was a risky thing but she couldn't help her impetuous nature. And who knew if she would ever get another chance like this again?

But surprisingly, Nate was the one to speak first.

"Lady Winchester, I apologize sincerely but at this stage in time, it is not feasible for a lady to work for the W.O. There are those who are constantly rallying against women equality in the Office as well and though I am not one of them, I am also not in the position to go against my superiors. But I promise you, if such a development were to occur, you shall be the first to be notified."

At her defeated look, however, he spoke again.

"But there is another possibility for your ladyship, and I suggest you speak with James here tonight, before making any decision. I shall sent word with James when he visits tomorrow. Now I bid you farewell, my lady." Bowing courteously over her hand, he was gone after one pointed look at both friends, still standing with comically shocked expressions on their faces.

"Connie I think you should depart to George's to celebrate another successful mission. I on the other hand, need to have a discussion with my wife." Conrad furrowed his brows at the abrupt dismissal, but decided to forgive his friend this once.

"See you tomorrow then, Jamie boy. It was a pleasure, Olivia." So saying, he left, leaving the pair alone in the Rose salon.

"So where were we? Ah yes, I believe I was just about to-",he began with a mysterious look on his face, but was cut off midway by a very alarmed Olivia.

"My lord, your mother is alone in your study, shouldn't we go to her? We most definitely shouldn't leave her there all alone, she must be bored waiting for so long! How terribly rude of me!" ,taking up handfuls of her cotton skirts, Olivia rushed out, not even looking behind to ascertain whether James followed her or not.

"This discussion is by no means over, Olivia! You cannot avoid it for long anyway.... I shall see to it that you don't. Olivia James Richardson!" James thundered after her, lowering his voice slightly when he noticed the servants staring at him, stupefied at their employer's behavior.

"There is nothing to see here all of you! Get back to your work!" James felt the heat creep up his neck as he spoke, and the maids and footmen sprang into action immediately, leaving him free to proceed to his study.

At the door, he realized he was still apprehensive of seeing his mother, even after the 'heart to heart' they had shared just an hour ago. Brushing off his sudden mood, he entered to find his wife and mother sitting next to each other on the diwan, looking like they were slowly getting used to each other. He wondered what they had said to each other to relax in each other's company.

His mother looked at him with eyes that were slightly rimmed in red. She had cried? He tried to suppress the instinctual need to comfort. Olivia motioned him closer to them and he almost refused, but what was the harm? It wasn't as if he was -

"I am leaving for the States tomorrow, James. I have secured passage on a vessel called The Libertine which sails at dawn. I - I had to see you before I left." Eunice took a few deep breaths, praying the tears would not spill before the son who would think her cowardly for them.

"I know you condemn what I did, James. But please, if you have any fond memories of your childhood with me, I beg of you to hear my last humble request to you. I shall never ask you for anything for the rest of my days, I promise you. Just one request."

James looked at the frail woman, who had recently been widowed, holding back her tears and pleading to her son to grant just one request before she left for a faraway continent, probably never to see him again, and his resolve to stay impassive crumbled in a second.

He did not even care if he was making a mistake by listening to her. She was his mother, even though they had been estranged for 21 years.

Kneeling at her feet to take Eunice's hands in his own, James said," Tell me what it is, mother, and I shall try my best to fulfill it. I give you my word." James looked at his mother reassuringly, trying to let her know it would all be alright.

Wiping the tears that finally spilled over, Eunice Marchbanks softly uttered something that left James speechless, and Olivia to just swallow uncomfortably and close her eyes in acceptance.

It was no use refusing. James had already given his word.

****

Later, after her mother-in-law had left the house in a hired hackney after a teary farewell and a large amount of apologizing on her part, Olivia turned to her Pirate. Looking at the sadness and grudging acknowledgement on his face, she smiled.

"We can do this James. We have stood up and defeated a national traitor, this will definitely be easier." Olivia enthused.

"Speaking of that, what exactly did you mean by telling Nate you wanted to join the W.O.? " James growled.

Olivia sighed. "I'm sorry James, I know I should have spoken with you before making that decision, but when I saw Mr. Nathaniel, I couldn't stop myself. It could very well have been my first and last chance to speak to him! But James, I really, really do wish to work as an agent.

I know it is not fun and games, risking your life out there to defend your country, so do not tell me I don't understand. It's just that.... I admire you for your courage, I really do. When I saw you after both my 'accidents', thinking about all the possibilities, narrowing your options, calculating, and just completely immersing yourself in your task, I knew that being an agent is in your blood. It is a way for you to channel your energy, your focus and your sense of justice.

I am inspired to use my intellect like you. I know that I probably will never get a chance to do so because I am a woman, but I couldn't not try! I would never forgive myself if I did not at least try!" She turned her bright eyes on her husband, beseeching him to understand.

"I don't suppose you know how proud I am of you, do you? Since you seem to know so much already!" James cupped her cheek tenderly, while she blushed at his statement.

Smiling at her reaction, he continued ,"Olivia, there is much more to consider before you become a spy, there are reasons women are not allowed to take this job, and even though a majority of these rules are pure bullshit, excuse my language, but a few are actually correct and worth considering. But since you are so passionate about it, I shall see what Nate tells me tomorrow, and we shall think about then. For now, I have something else I would rather do."

Reading his intention clearly in those brilliant grey eyes, Olivia felt the blood rush to her cheeks, hastily covering them with her hands. But James was not going to let that happen. He gently pulled her hands from her cheeks and brought them to his lips, kissing the underside of her wrist lingeringly, inhaling the floral scent that was an essential part of her while watching her eyes turn a darker shade of green, her breath hitching at his touch.

Olivia would never know why just a soft kiss from him made her so brazen, but she cast the thought away as she stood on her toes to peck him on the lips.

But before he could pull her in for a deeper, and certainly more satisfying kiss, she stopped him with a hand on his chest. Looking into the grey eyes that had intrigued her since she had first seen them, she decided to risk her heart.

"James-" Before she could say anything further, James shushed her, and concentrating on her confused face, said four words.

"Zoë mou, sas agapo."

He looked so vulnerable and hopeful, that it took Olivia a few seconds to process the Greek phrase.

My life, I love you.

Nothing could have stopped the tears that blurred her vision, as she jumped into the arms of her husband, raining kisses on his face. Byron, again.

"I love you", they both said simultaneously, beatific smiles on both their faces as they gazed at each other, content not to say another word.

Eventually, James carried her up the stairs to their bedchamber, and Olivia knew in her heart then, that her life was now complete. Everything else would sort out itself if she had her Pirate by her side.

Just before they crossed the threshold, James said quietly, "My Siren, I shall love you till the breath leaves my body, and if the Gods allow it, even after that happens."

Undone, Olivia kissed him with all the love, hope, happiness, and every shred of joy in her heart, which he reciprocated.

Now they knew nothing would be too great for them to overcome, no mountain to high, no valley too deep, no distance too far.

As long as they had each other.

Epilogue

London, 1809.

Olivia felt her hands slacken their hold on her mother and Elizabeth' s hands, and with a sigh of relief, she closed her eyes and let her head rest against the mountain of pillows at her back. As a baby's insistent wail filled the room, she smiled and opened her eyes, to see the midwife swaddle the child carefully and hand it to its proud grandmother.

Violet cooed softly to the infant in her arms, eyes glistening with unshed tears, as she walked to Olivia's side and handed the soft bundle to her. "You have a son, Olivia! A handsome little boy! What shall you call him?"

Just then the door was veritably torn from its hinges as a harried-looking James stood in the doorway, looking as if he hadn't slept a wink for days. Olivia smiled tremulously at her husband and said," Ethan Conrad Richardson, mama. That is what we shall call him. And he shall grow to become just as handsome and fearless as his papa."

Violet nodded at her daughter, smiling gently. Elizabeth wiped Olivia's brow one last time before kissing her cheek and whispering, "Congratulations Livvy! He truly is a handsome boy." Both women silently left the new parents to their privacy, closing the door with a quiet click.

James had walked a few steps into the room, still staring at his wife and newborn child as if he feared they would vanish like the mist in the morning if he dared to blink his eyes. Olivia's contractions had started the previous night, when all the family members, including Olivia's parents, Oliver, Elizabeth, Jane, and Conrad, had been lounging in the library at Bentham Park after dinner.

Though he had insisted he would remain at her side throughout the birthing, he was such a nervous wreck by the end of the first three hours, that the Duchess had ordered him out of the room, telling him to go 'drink some whiskey or go play some damn cards!', before slamming the door in his face.

He had spent the next twelve hours wearing a path in the carpet outside the room and the one in his study. The terror of losing her in the birthing had been eating at his heart since she had announced she was with child, but the pain had intensified a thousand-fold as he waited for word that she and the child were safe.

So, as soon as he heard the wail of his child through the closed door, he had desperately knocked down the door, only to see his strong, beautifully flushed wife holding a tiny swaddled bundle in her arms. On seeing him, she had given him a watery smile, before saying their child's name aloud. Just then James was swamped with the realization that-

She was alive! They had a son! And he was a father!

As the door shut behind him, he felt a tear spill over from the weight of his relief. "Oh, James!" Olivia sighed, and he saw that she too was crying silently. He was at her side in an instant, pulling her half onto his lap, and enclosing both her and the child in his arms.

Looking at his child, he saw eyes the same as his own peering at him through a veil of dark lashes. The feeling of seeing the tiny life that he and Olivia had created out of their love for each other almost overwhelmed him.

Olivia took his hand, bringing it near the grasping fingers of their child, and said," Ethan, this is your Papa. Say hello, darling." James looked awed at the mite-sized fingers that held his ring finger, but smoothed his other hand over his son's head carefully, reveling at the soft black down covering it.

"Olivia, I love you for so many reasons, and you have just given me one more. I do not know what I would have done if you were - were-", he could not bring himself to finish the sentence.

But Olivia shushed him, turning her head to face him, and placed a kiss on his cheek," Hush, my love. We are both healthy and well, you mustn't think of such dark thoughts around our child. But I must say, he looks just like you, my Pirate, if not more handsome." A smile dimpled her cheeks as James lowered his head to take her lips in a dangerously tender kiss, one that stole her breath away.

But Ethan had other plans. Letting out a lusty cry, he let his parents know that he was very hungry, indeed. As Olivia let him suckle at her breast, James remarked, "You must know that at this very moment, I envy our son very much."

Olivia felt her cheeks turn red. A year and a half of marriage and he could still make her blush like a newlywed!

"James!" she squeaked indignantly. Her husband, however, laughed loudly and pulled her closer, kissing the top of her head. He had never known such joy in his life as he had since Olivia had entered it, making everything more bright with her innate spark and positive nature. In a way, his father's selfish actions had helped him to have a blessed life.

****

After Ethan had been put to bed, Olivia and James proceeded to the dining room where their family awaited their arrival. Olivia, garbed in a gown of red silk with jacquard work along its length, stayed close to James, whose attire complimented her own, and was equally loathe to have any distance between them.

As the footmen opened the doors to the dining room, the Duke, Oliver, and Connie stood up politely, while the three women in attendance beamed at them. As soon as they were seated, the Duke, Olivia's father, stood up.

"I propose a toast," everyone stood at this announcement, raising their wine glasses, "to the Earl and Countess of Winchester, and their heir, Ethan Conrad Richardson. May their lives be filled with joy unsurmountable, and love never-ending."

There was a chorus of agreement as glasses clinked together.

"Thank you all for your kind wishes," said James and Olivia in unison, and motioned to the footmen to begin serving the first course.

****

Later, while the men retired to the study, Olivia and the women went up to the newly refurbished nursery, that had previously been Olivia's bedchamber, and after Olivia fed the restless Ethan, the Duchess fussed over her grandson for a bit before she declared that she would be retiring for a short nap before tea.

Jane smiled at Olivia. "Olivia, could I stay with Ethan for a while? I adore children, especially babies! Will it be alright?"The younger woman asked, with her habitual shyness.

"Of course, Jane. But if he falls asleep, lay him down in the crib, alright?" Olivia smiled at her sister-in-law, James's sister before exiting the room with Elizabeth.

"So, no more missions for a few months, right Liv?" smirked Elizabeth. She, Olivia and Grace worked for a mysterious society matron as Lady spies, and the months of training that Beth and Grace had given her, had helped their friendship to blossom into a strong one.

Olivia had got her wish when James had told her about the information Nate had sent through him. The Matron, or M as she was called, was a well-respected lady of the ton, but her name had been withheld for obvious reasons. Under her guidance, five ladies of the ton, Olivia being the only married one, helped solve crimes in London that involved rather valuable artifacts.

Such crimes occurred more often than one would think, and the five delighted in their job. But with the birth of Ethan, Olivia would essentially be 'off duty' for a year, at least till she could leave him with a nursemaid for a few hours at a time.

But she was not disheartened, her baby boy was more important than being a spy.

Giving her friend a sly look, she asked," But darling, don't you want to settle down yourself? I know that gentlemen are clamoring to stand in line for your hand, do you want to disappoint so many of them?"

Beth's greyish-blue eyes flashed to her green ones before she hastily replied," I have no one I wish to tie myself to for eternity, Liv. It is more than likely I'll end up at a convent than marry or even a spinster with ten dogs."

"Oh, but I thought Con-," Olivia started, only to be interrupted by her friend with a simple reply.

"Please, Livvy. I do not wish to go down that road today."

Olivia nodded in mute understanding. Men could be thickheaded fools sometimes, especially when emotions were involved. But she knew she would not rest until she had tried to get her friends together. James had warned her against meddling, but this would not be the first time she had disregarded her husband's opinion.

Mentally rubbing her hands with glee, Olivia started to tell her friend of the modiste that was coming to the house the next day, to take her measurements for a few new gowns, as the season came closer.

Though she replied with enthusiasm, Elizabeth was inwardly cursing herself, and that damnably handsome rogue, Conrad Brighton. But there was nothing to be done for it now.

She had made a mistake, and she would have to bear the consequences.

And to hell with those compelling green eyes.

Lightning Source UK Ltd.
Milton Keynes UK
UKHW020440211122
412554UK00016B/811